SEARCHING FOR RAVEN

To: Caleb

Happy Reading

Searching for Raven

Jerry Hines

NORTH STAR PRESS OF ST. CLOUD, INC.
St. Cloud, Minnesota

To my mother, the teacher.

Although she is no longer with us,
she is a part of every word I write.

Copyright © 2014 Jerry Hines
Cover art by Patrycja Ignaczak

ISBN 978-0-87839-736-5

First Edition, June 2014

Printed in the United States of America

Published by
North Star Press of St. Cloud, Inc.
P.O. Box 451
St. Cloud, MN 56302

www.northstarpress.com

~1~

The young Indian boy stood on the porch railing, looking east where the bright summer sun just began to creep over the top of the pine trees on the horizon. In another couple of hours it would be hot—very hot—and now would be the best time to do his chores, before the heat of the day.

He was almost eleven years old, but small for his age—weighing just seventy pounds. The top of his jet-black hair barely cleared the highest rail of the wooden fence that kept the cattle from going astray.

Turning, he slowly placed one bare foot in front of the other on the porch rail, being careful not to slip off the four-inch-wide board. He pretended he was walking a cliff above the great Superior Lake he and his grandpa had visited. He needed to be very careful with each step, so he wouldn't fall onto imagined jagged rocks protruding from the lake's surface hundreds of feet below. He kept his balance by holding his arms straight out from his sides. When he reached the corner of the porch, he stopped. He lifted his right leg until it was perpendicular to his body. After holding it there for only a second, he slowly bent his left leg then pushed hard, jumping straight up into the air. In one fluid motion, he twisted his body and landed on on the rail, his right leg in exactly the same spot, facing the opposite direction. The boy smiled with satisfaction.

He looked out into the field, where the cattle already started to gather around the feeding trough, waiting for their daily ration of grain. Then he noticed a bird soaring high above the grassy terrain. He glanced at his arms still sticking straight out from his body—like spread wings—and thought, *I wish I could soar like a bird*. He watched the bird intently, trying to draw its attention, then he dropped his right arm slightly.

A few seconds later the bird dropped its right wing and began to descend toward the farm. The boy lifted his right arm back up and the bird did the same with its wing. The boy dropped his left arm slightly and immediately the bird did that with its left wing . . .

"Kian!" a voice hollered from inside the house. "Are you still in the bathroom? You can't stay in there all day, you know. There are chores to be done."

Startled, the boy dropped both of his arms, nearly falling off the rail. "No, Pop-o, I'm on the front porch. I was just getting ready to feed the cattle. Should I give them both grain and hay today?"

"What day is it today, Kian?"

The boy scratched his head, searching for the answer. "Wednesday . . . I think."

"You think right for a change," his father teased. "And what do the cattle get every Wednesday?"

Kian jumped off the rail onto the porch, then lowered his head and dropped his voice to almost a whisper. "Grain *and* hay, I guess." He edged this with sarcasm because he didn't think his father would hear.

"You guessed correctly," his father said, as he stepped out onto the porch, startling Kian again. This time Kian almost fell off the step.

"Oh, Pop-o! You scared me."

The boy jumped off the porch, landing on the hard clay. In the same swift motion he did a summersault, then came right to his feet and turned toward his father. "Are ya going to work on Mr. Kessler's roof again today?"

"Yes, Kian. I'll be leaving soon."

Kian worded his next question carefully. "When I finish my chores, can I ride Raven?"

"Yes, you can ride Raven, but only after *all* the chores are done," his father answered. Before Kian could ask the next question about riding him bareback, his father continued. "And, yes, you can ride him bareback, but, you need to be careful. Do you understand?"

Kian grew a smile from ear to ear. "Yes, Pop-o, I understand. I'll be careful, I promise. And I'll get all my chores done first."

Raven, a beautiful black gelding, had belonged to Kian's mother. She had died just over six months ago. She had named the horse after the birds so common in the area. His mother had taught him how to ride Raven when he was just six years old. Kian believed his mother could ride better than anyone he knew. Sometimes, when Kian closed his eyes he could see his mother's long, black hair flowing behind her as she laid her body against Raven's back and flew like the wind across the open field. She'd taught Kian to ride bareback and he was very good at it.

After Kian's mother died, Raven had stayed in the shed a long time before Kian was allowed to ride him. Pop-o would go out to the shed, close the door and spend hours with the horse, but would never ride him. He groomed him and talked to him, but never ride. Kian didn't understand why. He guessed it was because Raven used to be his mother's horse. Riding him might bring back memories too painful for his father.

One day, about three months after Kian's mother passed away, Pop-o had come home from work and found Kian sitting on Raven. Kian was resting his head against Raven's neck and whispering something. Kian didn't hear his father come into the shed, but after a few minutes he sat up and noticed his father.

"Mother has been speaking with me again," Kian said. "She told me she wishes we'd start to ride Raven. She said it's time." Kian knew his father understood him when he said his mother had been speaking to him, because her spirit had spoken to him before.

~ ~ ~ ~ ~

Kian's mother and father had found out there was something special about Kian at a very young age—that he had almost magical power. He was able to communicate with the spirits of their ancestors. And when Kian was only six or seven years old, they found out he could communicate with birds. At first they didn't think too much of this because it wasn't like he actually talked to them. But he showed them he could get birds to understand what he wanted them to do. And they did it.

The first time Kian told his parents this, they just laughed. They saw no harm in letting him have his make-believe world. But then, one day, he showed them that it really was true.

"I can tell that robin to fly around the shed and land on my head," Kian said in his most serious voice.

"All right then," his father teased, "we're watching."

Kian jumped off the porch and ran toward the fence where the robin perched. The robin never moved as Kian approached. The boy stood in front of the robin a few seconds then lifted his right hand. The bird flew from the fence, circled the shed and landed on Kian's head. Kian lifted his left arm, and the bird took off from his head, flew around the shed in the opposite direction, and landed on the same spot, only this time desposited something in Kian's hair. Kian's parents laughed when they saw the white goop run down the side of his head. but they began to realize Kian had something special.

Not long after, Kian started telling his mother things. They were things that happened to her ancestors she knew but had never talked to Kian about before.

"How do you know these things?" his mother asked.

Kian told her the spirits spoke to him about many things. He and his mother had long conversations about her parents and ancestors and about things from long ago.

After Kian's mother died, Kian told his father he was able to communicate with his mother's spirit. He said it was the same as with the birds: that he didn't actually hear her voice, but he heard her in his head.

~ ~ ~ ~ ~

Kian brought feed to the cattle while his father prepared the truck to leave. He watched his father carry the large toolbox from the shed. His father was a strong man with a solid muscular build. Well over six feet tall, his dark, tanned skin looked bronze in the morning sun. Kian noticed streaks of gray in his black hair that hadn't been there before—before his mother died.

That was just one change Kian had noticed in his father over the past six months. For a long time his father had been quieter. Many evenings he would just sit on the porch and stare out into space. Kian felt his father's pain.

When Kian's mother was still alive, his father had been different. Many days, when his father came home from work, Kian would be standing by the steps that led upstairs. When his father walked in the door, Kian would say, "I'm the toughest Indian around. I can ride any horse alive."

His father would respond, "Oh, yeah? Well let's see you ride this one." He'd turn so Kian could jump on his back, then he grabbed Kian's legs and pretended he was a bucking bronco. The two of them would laugh so loud sometimes Kian's mother came to see what all the noise was about. That seemed like such a long time ago.

Ever since his father let Kian ride Raven, things got a little better. His father seemed a bit happier and showed more interest in Kian and Raven. Kian hoped one day he'd be able to get Pop-o to ride Raven again. Then maybe he and Pop-o would share the happiness they used to have. He wanted so much for Pop-o to come home from work and wrestle with him in the front room, or ride with him and Grandpa to the river and streams and fish or swim. He couldn't remember the last time Pop-o asked him to play catch. All of these things Kian missed so much.

Kian walked to his father with a few kernels of corn in his hand. A small chipmunk a short distance behind him watched. When Kian spoke with his father, the chipmunk stayed a safe distance away.

"Let me show you what I taught that chipmunk."

His father smiled. "Okay, if it doesn't take long."

"See the fence over by the shed?" Kian nodded his head toward the house. "Which of the four fence posts should I tell my little friend to go sit on?"

Pop-o scratched his head. "I guess it doesn't matter. Any one of them."

Kian said, "But it does matter. You have to tell me which one, otherwise you might think I planned this ahead of time. So which one?"

"Okay then, the one on the far right."

Kian turned around and bent over. As soon as he did, the striped critter ran to him and ate a kernel of the corn. After a few seconds, Kian stood up and faced the fence. Immediately, the chipmunk ran over to it and climbed up the post on the far right and sat on the top.

Kian's father smiled, then put the rest of his things in the truck, got in and started it. When Kian came over and stood by the truck, Pop-o reached out the window and ruffled up his son's long hair.

"If you plan to go to your grandfather's tomorrow, you better send your little friend home and make sure you get everything done today." Then he put the truck in gear and started down the rutted path that served as their farm road, waving once to Kian, but never looking back.

Kian stood there for a long time, watching his father drive down their half-mile dirt road, then turn at the lonesome oak tree that marked the northwest corner of their property.

~ 2 ~

Kian decided he'd better at least finish feeding the cattle before he rode Raven this morning. He hurried back to the shed to get the rest of the feed. He could finish the rest of the chores after his ride.

Once the cattle were fed, Kian went back to the shed and prepared Raven for his morning ride. Kian was eager to practice the trick he had been working on with Raven for that past week. He knew he could never show it to Pop-o until he could do it perfectly.

He led Raven into the fenced area where the cattle were kept. The ground was softer and level there—just in case he fell.

He jumped on Raven's back, laid his head next to Raven's neck and whispered, "Okay, Raven let's go."

Raven took off like a streak of lightning as Kian melted into his neck and back so the two of them seemed to be one creature, racing across the field. When they got about two hundred yards away, Kian pulled on the reins, and Raven came to a screeching stop.

"Okay, Raven, you know what to do. Bring us back nice and easy, so I can do this trick."

Raven galloped slowly, back toward the fence. At the halfway point, Kian slowly pushed his body away from Raven's neck. Still holding the reins, he lifted his leg and placed his right foot in the middle of Raven's lower back. Raven continued at an even pace, and Kian was ready to complete the trick.

He needed to lift his other foot and place it on Raven's back, so he could stand up. The last two times he had tried, he stood only halfway before he became scared and sat back down. He was determined to make it all the way up today.

Placing his other foot on Raven's back, Kian rode in a crouch position for a short way before he finally pushed his legs and stood straight up. Kian smiled. He held the reins tightly as he rode back to the fence.

"WHOA, RAV . . ." was all Kian could get out before he came tumbling off Raven's back and hit the ground. "Oooph"

Kian had just noticed the gopher, running in front of Raven when the horse lifted his head and broke stride just enough to throw Kian off his back. Kian had summersaulted into a half-roll before hitting the ground and the fence with his shoulder and the side of his face.

He lay on his back with his eyes closed for what seemed like minutes, but was actually only a few seconds. When he opened his eyes, he looked straight up at the puffy white clouds and blue sky. He closed his eyes a few more seconds. When he opened his eyes again, Raven's big face appeared over him. Kian tried to smile, but when he did, it hurt his face. So much for perfecting his new riding trick today.

A little later, Kian stood in his father's bedroom, looking in the mirror above the dresser, trying to clean dirt out of the torn flesh of his face. While holding some bandages against the scrape, he looked at the picture of his mother on the dresser. A tear worked its way out of the corner of his eye and down the side of his face into the open wound—stinging a little. He missed her so much.

~ ~ ~ ~ ~

Kian was almost ten and a half when his mother died. His memories of how she died were not clear. Many times Kian had wanted to ask his father about it, but he never did. He feared if he did, it might make his father sad and maybe he would start drinking again.

All Kian remembered was that his mother got real sick. He didn't know how she got sick or what kind of sickness it was, but she was sick for a long time. Then one day . . . she was gone. He remembered the doctor came only once after she had become very sick. Soon after that visit, he remembered, his father had started to drink.

Before the doctor's visit, Kian would go in to see his mother every day, sit with her and talk to her. She would ask him about his day. He would tell her all about how he helped his father or how he got to ride Raven. His mother loved it when he told her about riding Raven.

When Kian's mother was young, she'd loved to ride horses and became an excellent rider. Kian's grandfather said she could ride as well as or better, than any of the Indian braves.

"Someday, Mama, I'll ride Raven as good as you. I'll ride him bareback all the time. I'll be as good a rider as you are. You just wait and see. I'll show you."

"I know, little man," she said, "You'll always make me proud." Kian liked it when she called him "little man." It made him feel bigger than he actually was.

She closed her eyes a moment and then said, "You do know, Kian, that I will always love you. You do know that, don't you?"

"Of course, Mama," was all he could say. That was the last thing he remembered his mother saying.

Mama wasn't with them very long after that. He remembered his father and the doctor whispering in the bedroom, away from his mother, so she couldn't hear. And then he remembered seeing his father cry—only for a very short time though. It was the only time he had seen his father cry.

~ ~ ~ ~ ~

12

The loud screech of a raven high up in the sky, brought Kian out of his daze. Kian looked out the bedroom window at the sun, which was getting higher in the sky. He knew he had better finish the rest of his chores if he was going to have them done by the time his father got home.

~ 3 ~

The sound of a distant train whistle made Kian step out from behind the shed and look off to the south. *It must be after five o'clock*, he thought. As the train slowly moved on the horizon, Kian squinted in the direction of the track. He put one hand over his eyes to shield them from the sun and searched.

Finally, he spotted a dot, moving in front of the distant pines, not far from where the train had passed, and he knew it was his father. Kian figured in only about fifteen minutes his father would be home. He finished fixing the last broken board behind the shed, then collected his tools. He went into the house to start supper.

Looking out the kitchen window, Kian watched Pop-o park the truck next to the shed. His father took out his neckerchief and wiped the sweat from his brow. Kian hoped Pop-o wasn't too tired. He didn't want him to be upset when he saw the scrape on his face. He hoped the smell of fresh cornbread might put his father in a better mood when he came into the kitchen.

Kian had finished all his chores, just as he was supposed to. When Pop-o walked into the kitchen and greeted his son, Kian was setting the table for supper, trying to keep the side of his face away from his father.

"It looks like you did a good job cleaning the living room and kitchen. Is the rest of the house as clean?"

"Yes, Pop-o, I cleaned the whole house like I was supposed to." He continued to set the table, hoping his father wouldn't see his face just yet. "I made cornbread. Can you smell it in the oven?"

"It smells terrific," his father answered. "I'll get cleaned up, and finish making supper so we can eat."

When Kian's father left the kitchen, Kian gave a sigh of relief. But he knew that sooner or later his father would see his scraped-up face.

Twenty minutes later, Kian's father finished making one of their favorite meals—fish, wild rice, greens, and cornbread. Kian's father liked fish better than anything. Kian's favorite was wild rice. They both loved cornbread.

"Kian! Kian, come down. Supper is ready," Pop-o hollered.

Kian had been waiting right outside the kitchen door and stepped in, catching his father by surprise. "I'm right here, Pop-o," he said.

"Oh! My word! What happened to your face?" Kian's father immediately went to his son, grabbing his chin and turning his face to have a better look at the scrape. "How did this happen?"

Kian looked down at the floor. When his father let go of his chin, he said, "I fell off of Raven this morning," almost in a whisper.

Kian's father was silent a long time. Finally, Pop-o asked. "Is there anything else you'd like to add to that?"

Kian knew what his father was asking. He hoped he wouldn't have to tell him about trying to stand on Raven's back. Kian also knew he couldn't lie to Pop-o. He never was any good at lying. When he was very young, whenever he tried to lie, his face turned red and his throat became dry. His mother had said that was a good quality, but Kian sometimes thought differently. Right then he wished he could stretch the truth a little, but he was sure Pop-o would know.

"I was trying to do a trick while I was riding Raven and a stupid gopher ran in front of him. When Raven tried to miss the gopher, I fell off him."

Again there was a long pause before Pop-o said, "And this trick, are you going to tell me about the wonderful trick that made your face look like raw hamburger?"

Kian tried not to smile, but it was hard. "I was trying to ride Raven, standing on his back."

Kian's father went over to the stove and brought the food to the table for supper.

Kian sat in his place. After a few moments of silence, he finally asked, "Are you mad at me, Pop-o?"

His father thought awhile before answering. "No, Kian, I'm not *mad* at you. I am disappointed. You don't seem to realize how serious this could have been. I'm not upset you tried a new trick with Raven. I'm upset you tried it when I wasn't home. If you had been seriously hurt, there was no one here to help you."

He dished up some wild rice and passed the bowl to Kian before he continued. "You're old enough now to know what you can and can't do when I'm not here. Do you understand, Kian?"

Kian looked down at his plate and stirred his food with his fork, and said, "Yes, Pop-o." After a few more seconds he added, "I'm sorry, Pop-o."

The two of them were quiet for the better part of the meal. Then Pop-o changed the subject by asking Kian some questions about the trip he was planning to take with his grandfather. He wanted to know what they planned to do and what Kian would be taking and if he had packed everything. It wasn't long before Kian felt that things were back to normal again.

~ 4 ~

Kian's grandfather, Taza, was full-blooded Ojibwa. Raised on a reservation in northern Minnesota, Taza's mother and father had been killed when he was only three years old. The rest of the tribe raised Taza after his parents died. Kian wondered if he and his grandfather were so close because they'd both lost their mothers at a young age.

Kian knew Taza was somewhere between seventy and seventy-five years old. He had long straight hair that he tied in a ponytail at the base of his neck. It was probably black at one time, but for as long as Kian could remember, Taza's hair had been silver.

He lived by himself on a piece of property about three miles from Kian and his father. Kian didn't remember much about his grandmother. She had died when Kian was only two. His mother told him once that she had a brother. Her brother moved out east to go to school. No one had heard from him since. Kian hoped someday his grandfather would tell Kian all about him.

Taza still lived in the same two-room shanty where he had raised his two children. No running water or electricity—in many ways, he still lived the same way as his ancestors had when he was growing up.

Whenever Kian had the chance to ride his horse with his grandfather, he would ask to ride bareback. That was how his grandfather used to ride. "When you were my age, Grandpa, did you ride bareback all the time?"

"Of course I did," his grandpa answered, "I was never lucky enough to have a saddle."

"How come you don't ride bareback anymore?"

"At my age you need something more than just your backside to stay on the horse," he said with a smile.

Kian also tried to speak his native tongue with Taza, even though he only knew a small amount of Ojibwa. He wanted so much to be like his grandfather.

He stayed with his grandfather several times each year. His grandfather shared many stories about Kian's ancestors. Each time Taza told Kian a new story, Kian was mesmerized by what his grandfather said.

"When I grow up, I want to be an Indian warrior like my ancestors," Kian would say.

"When you grow up, you need to finish school, go to college, and study to be a doctor or a lawyer. That's what you need to do," his grandfather would answer.

Kian had heard this from Taza before. He always asked Kian how school was going. When Kian told him,

"It's okay," Taza would answer, "You need to do better than okay if you want to go to college."

Of course, when Taza said that, Kian would say, "but what if I don't want to go to college?"

Then Taza would tease Kian by answering, "Then Kian will be a knucklehead just like his grandpa." Kian liked it when his grandpa teased him.

Kian would be spending the weekend with his grandfather. Kian's father had business in Grand Marais, which was a long way from their farm, so he wouldn't be back until late Sunday. What made this visit extra special was that his grandfather had promised to take Kian on a trip to the rocky cliffs of the great Lake Superior.

Kian rode the rocky uneven terrain along the base of Lake Superior—a trail which led to his grandfather's property. His house was set on the highest part of the property and on a clear day he could see Lake Superior, way off in the distance. There was a small marshy pond on the opposite end of his property. More than once Kian had spotted a moose drinking from it. When he came to the clearing that opened up to his grandfather's property, he gently nudged Raven with his heels to let the horse know he should pick up the pace. The whole time since they had left home, Kian had kept Raven at a slow trot so he would have plenty of energy left for the last half mile. He wanted to show his grandfather how fast Raven had become.

He hoped his grandfather would be outside working and would see them when they came through the clearing. That's when he decided to let Raven fly.

"Come on, Raven," he whispered in the horse's ear, "Let's show my grandpa what you can do."

Raven picked up his pace until he was running at a full gallop. Kian wrapped one arm around Raven's neck, and it almost seemed like he became part of the horse. Out of the corner of his eye, Kian saw his grandpa chopping wood behind the house. He was glad because then his grandpa would see how well he could ride.

"Ooooo, eeee yhaaaa!" Kian yelled as he passed through the gate of his grandfather's property. He pulled on the reins, and Raven came to a stop three feet in front of his grandfather.

"Hi, Grandpa." Kian smiled as he threw one of his legs over Raven's back. He sat there for a moment with his hands on his chin and his elbows on his knees. "Did you see how well I can ride Raven? Isn't he fast, Grandpa?"

"Yes, Kian. Raven is very fast and you ride him well. How long did it take you to get here?"

Kian thought for a moment, and then said, "About twenty minutes, I think."

Taza rubbed his chin and Kian could tell he was trying to figure something out. Finally, he said, "Good that means you were smart enough not to ride Raven fast and hard all the way here. That would not be good for him."

"I only rode him fast from the edge of the clearing. I didn't want to get him too tired out."

Kian jumped off Raven's back and grabbed the reins. The two of them walked around to the front of the house, where Kian removed Raven's saddle and brought him water. He tied Raven to a post in the shade and sat down on the large wooden swing on the porch. When Taza came out of the house with a cold drink, he noticed Kian's face.

"What happened to the side of your face, boy?" Taza took Kian's chin in his hand and turned it so he could have a better look. "These scrapes wouldn't be from doing some kind of trick with your friend over there, would they?" he said, pointing at Raven.

Kian looked embarrassed and tried to turn his face away. At first he wasn't going to tell his grandpa what happened, but Taza would get it out of him sooner or later. He said, "I was trying to ride Raven standing up when a stupid gopher spooked him and I fell off."

"I'm not sure the gopher is the stupid one. I'll bet his face isn't all scraped up like yours."

Kian admitted, "Your probably right, Grandpa."

He and Taza spent the next half hour talking about their trip. Kian had a million questions, and Taza tried to answer all of them. Even if a question was silly or repetitious, Taza would still answer it.

When Kian's questions ran out the two of them sat for a long time—silent. Taza studied Kian's face and knew that the boy had something on his mind, but waited until Kian was ready to talk about it.

Kian looked into his grandpa's eyes, searching for answers before he even asked a question. Finally, he spoke. "Grandpa, do I really have special powers? I mean, you know, do you really think I can hear my mother's voice in my head or the voices of our ancestors? And am I really able to communicate with birds and animals?"

"It doesn't matter what I think," he said. "And it doesn't matter what anybody else thinks. What matters is what you *believe*."

Taza stood and said he had to finish chopping wood. Kian watched as Taza lifted the large ax with his muscular arms and buried its head deep into the wood. *Whopp!* The ax tore into the wood. The smell of fresh chopped cedar reminded Kian of the time he helped Taza and his father build their shed. When Taza finished chopping, Kian helped by stacking the wood next to the porch. Once finished, they went in and began preparing for their trip to Lake Superior.

~ ~ ~ ~ ~

The next day, Kian and Taza set out. They rode side by side for the first half of their trip to the great lake's rocky base. The sun was almost directly over their heads as they rode the dusty trail. While they rode, Taza explained to Kian what was so special about where they were going.

"When I was your age, my tribal father—the Indian chief who raised me when my parents died—took me to this very spot on the cliffs where we're going today. It was later, when I was twelve or thirteen that he brought me back up here and explained the mystery of the Magic Sunrise. Today I will try to explain it to you"

Kian looked at his grandfather with eyes as big as saucers. "Will we see the Magic Sunrise today?" he asked. Sometimes Kian spoke before he thought.

Taza laughed out loud and looked at Kian with teasing eyes. "For such a smart, young, talented boy, you can be a knucklehead sometimes," Taza joked. "Now, think about what you just asked."

Kian scratched the top of his head, and looked down at Raven as if the horse might know what his grandfather meant. Just about ready to say something, he realized what his grandfather meant. "Oh, yeah! I get it. Sunrise's over. I guess I wasn't thinking, huh, Grandpa?"

His grandfather just laughed again, and they rode the rest of the way in silence.

It wasn't long that the trail narrowed, with large boulders on either side. They had to ride single file. Both horses had been on this trail before. Each took careful steps as they worked their way to the top. Taza led the way, looking back frequently to be sure Kian was safe.

The trip to the top took almost half an hour. They stopped once to rest the horses—at least, that's what

Taza told Kian why they stopped, but Kian wondered if it was so his grandfather could check on him. He knew his grandfather would never let anything happen to him.

When they neared the top, Taza slid off his horse. He tied the reins to a dogwood shrub and told Kian to do the same. Kian obeyed his grandfather but wondered why they'd stop when they weren't at the top yet. From where they stood, Kian could only see the blue sky above and the jagged boulders on either side of them. He thought they still must have a ways to go.

"Why are we stopping here, Grandpa? We're not at the top yet, are we?"

"Patience, little one," was all Taza said. He started to walk between two huge rocks. Kian followed.

In just a few minutes Kian realized why Taza didn't want to bring the horses. The path became narrow with sharp granite edges. The horses would have a difficult time. They climbed a series of rocks like big steps to a large, flat cliff that looked out over Lake Superior.

For a long time Kian studied the huge granite boulders with their sharp, cutting edges in the lake below. He watched as the thundering waves came rushing into shore completely submerging the angry, gray boulders, then gently receded, exposing the vicious rocks again. The opening where they stood was at the very top of the cliffs and looked like it had been carved out just for the purpose of viewing. It was only about ten feet long and six to eight feet wide. A three-foot piece of flat, smooth granite stuck out over the cliffs like a platform. Kian stepped out on the rock and looked down at the huge boulders and crashing waves, wondering if anyone could survive a fall from here. He looked at Taza with big round eyes. Taza knew Kian had many questions.

"This lake can be many things to different people," Taza said. "Some call it *angry waters* and others see it as peaceful and calm. It just dependeds on when you visit it. By the look in your eyes I'd say you don't think it's very peaceful. Am I right?"

Kian nodded, then continued to check out the rest of the beautiful view. Straight ahead, as far as the eye could see was water—it looked like an ocean. On the right, cliff formations made a large, sweeping, curved shoreline that ended at the tip of a peninsula. Kian studied those formations and found them interesting, because the cliffs appeared to get bigger the further away they were from him. He wondered if it was just an illusion. Many cliff formations seemed to butt up against each other like different-sized books on a shelf. One of the cliffs had an arch. The arch was very far away, so far it was hard to tell for sure if it actually was an arch.

While Kian was studying the formations, Taza stood next to him and said, "You seem interested in those cliff formations at the end of the peninsula. What can you tell me about them?"

"Well," Kian replied, "they look really neat, and it seems like one of them has an arch in it, but they are so far away it is hard to tell for sure."

"You're right, little one. There is an arch in one of them. That's what makes them so special. Now sit down and I will tell you why."

"What about the Magic Sunrise?"

"In time, boy, in time. Now sit and listen."

Taza began by telling Kian about the times he had ridden up here with his tribal father. Although Taza spent much of his time taking care of himself, his tribal father was always there to show him new adventures. This particular place became very special to Taza.

"When I was old enough, the chief told me we would make the trip to this very place early in the morning to see the Magic Sunrise. It was late September so we began the journey in the dark. As we climbed the rocks to get to this spot, I noticed it was starting to get light enough to see. I wondered if we might have missed the sunrise.

"The chief told me not to worry. He said, 'Even though the sun has risen in one person's horizon, it may not have yet risen in another's.' At the time, I wasn't sure what he meant. I soon found out. We stood on this cliff looking toward the peninsula." Taza pointed at the irregular formations with his gnarly, weathered hand. "'There,' the chief said to me, 'watch those rock formations closely.' I did. I wasn't sure what I was looking for, because the sky was already turning light, but I still couldn't see any sun, so I waited patiently. Then, in the middle of one of the taller rock formations, I thought I saw a glimmer of light. Suddenly, like a burst of magic, the bright sunlight came pouring through that arch in the middle of those rocks and bathed us in sunlight." Taza was still pointing and Kian followed his finger to what looked like an arch. "That is where you will see the Magic Sunrise."

Kian stood and watched the arch a long time, as if watching it might produce a second sunrise. Then Kian would get to witness the sunrise for himself.

Of course, it didn't happen, so, after a while, Kian looked at his grandfather and said, "Can we stay here tonight and watch the Magic Sunrise tomorrow?"

Taza put his hand on Kian's shoulder and laughed. "Sorry, little one, it wouldn't matter if we were here tomorrow at sunrise or the next day or all week. In fact, it wouldn't matter if we were here all month, because you see, there are only four days out of the year that the Magic Sunrise appears in this very spot. Now sit back down and let me explain."

Kian put his elbows on his knees and his face in his hands and studied his grandfather's weathered face as Taza told him the secret of the Magic Sunrise.

Taza began by asking Kian why it might have been light enough for them to see even though the sun hadn't appeared to rise yet. Kian wondered if the sun had been behind the cliffs so they couldn't see it. Taza told him he was right, and then explained how each day the sun rose from a different point on the horizon. After a lengthy explanation of how it rose more to the south in winter and then moves back to the north in the summer, Kian understood it rose in a slightly different spot each day.

"So you see, Kian, there are only two days in the spring and two days in the fall when the sun shines through that arch and bathes this small spot where we're standing with sunlight. On the third day, the sunshine will be over there, to our left, off the side of that cliff."

"So, which two days in fall does the Magic Sunrise appear?" Kian asked.

"At the end of September," Taza answered. "In fact, one of those days falls on your mother's birthday. That's another reason the Magic Sunrise is so special."

Kian sat for a long time, staring at the arch that helped create the Magic Sunrise. He wondered if his mother had ever seen it. Finally, he asked, "Will I ever get to see the Magic Sunrise Grandfather?"

"Yes, little one, I'm sure you will . . . someday."

Taza faced Kian. "You know this was one of your mother's favorite places in the whole world. She loved it here. She called this her little paradise."

Kian got up, walked to his grandfather, looked up at him. "Tell me more about my mother, Grandpa. Tell me what she was like when she was a little girl."

Taza looked down at Kian and sighed. He backed up a couple of steps and sat down on a rock. "Well," Taza started, "you already know she was a wonderful mother. Let me tell you what kind of girl she was. When she was little, she used to play tricks on your grandmother and me all the time. In fact, the first time she played a trick on us was when she was born. Your grandmother started having labor pains. I went for the doctor, but when we got back, she'd stopped having pains. The next day she did the very same thing. Two days later I went to get the doctor again, but this time when we got there, your mother was already born. I guess she just wanted to come out on her own.

"She used to get into all kinds of mischief—just like you at her age—and as soon as she learned how to walk, she wanted to ride a horse. She was too small to ride by herself, but I took her everywhere I went. When she got a little bigger, she used to pester me all the time to let her ride by herself. I told her she was too small, but one day I looked out the window to see she had brought my horse next to the porch. She stood on the rail and jumped on the horse's back. She tried to hold on to the horse's mane, but when it took a few steps, she fell off. Anyway, by the time she was six she was riding bareback all the time."

Kian listened intently, absorbing every bit of information his grandfather could give him.

When Taza had finished, Kian thought about the times he had tried to get his father to tell him about his mother, but his father just couldn't do it. Each time he would try, after a few moments, his father's eyes would glaze over and he would stop. Finally, he would say, "We'll talk about this another time," but they never did.

Kian dug the toe of his shoe into a crack in the rock and said, "Grandpa, will Pop-o ever be happy again?"

When Taza didn't answer right away, Kian said, "I tried to get him to tell me about my mother and what things were like before I was born, but he couldn't do it. I could tell it was too hard for him. I wonder if he'll ever feel like doing the things he used to do before . . . you know, before my mother died."

Taza waited before he spoke, glad Kian was sharing his feelings. Kian's head was turned down. Taza couldn't see his eyes, but he saw a tear fall from his chin.

Kian said, "It makes me sad Pop-o isn't happy like he used to be. I want so much for everything to be like it was before."

Kian laid his head in Taza's lap, and Taza stroked Kian's long, black hair. Finally, Taza spoke. "Your father is a very good man, son. He loved your mother very much, as he does you. When she died, a piece of him went with her. So your father has a hole in his heart that needs to heal before he can be himself again."

Taza was silent again for a while as he continued to stroke Kian's hair. Then he said, "An old Indian once told me, *the heart is the most important part of the body, because it feeds not only the body, but also the spirit and that is why it takes the longest to heal.* In time, my son, the hole in your father's heart will heal, and then things will be like they were before. I promise."

~ 5 ~

Taza stood up and told Kian it was time to go back. Kian went first, leading the way back down the path. About fifty yards from the horses, he heard them neighing. The sound was not the friendly sound Raven made when Kian approached him in the morning. It was more a sound of distress.

Kian looked back at Taza and saw the worried look on his grandpa's face and became worried himself. He turned back to the trail and started to hurry. He was running when he heard Taza yell, "Kian! Kian! Be careful!"

Kian kept on running. He heard his horse again.

"Raven! Raven I'm coming!" Kian yelled.

His feet barely touched the ground as he swiftly maneuvered around the rocks and crevices in the trail. His mind raced, trying to think what could be wrong.

Rounding the last large rock that kept him from seeing the horses, he realized the problem. Raven was trying to rise up on his hind legs but couldn't. The reins were tied too tightly to the bush where they had left him.

For a split second Kian did not know why Raven was acting that way. Then he saw the crouching bear in front of Raven, ready to pounce. Instinctively, Kian looked for a large rock or a stick he could use to defend Raven.

Kian heard his grandfather tell him to stay back. He didn't listen. He didn't want anything to happen to Raven. The black bear snarled and inched closer. Kian was sure if he didn't do something, the bear would attack. For one split second, he thought of trying to get the bear's attention and communicate with it as he did with birds and chipmunks, but he knew it didn't work with all animals especially if they felt they were in danger.

The thought of losing Raven blocked all others. He knew he had to act quickly. As Raven came down to the ground for the second time, Kian saw the bear move closer again. He had to untie Raven and pull him away.

"Kian, don't!" Taza yelled.

Just as Kian reached for the reins, the bear struck. Kian tried to kick at the bear's head, but the bear was quicker and sank its angry, sharp teeth into Kian's leg.

"Ouweee!" cried Kian. He backed up and reached for his leg in pain while the bear stood its ground, snarling, crouching into attack position again. Kian feared that the bear would go for Raven, but all he could do was fall to the ground and watch.

He wondered why Taza wasn't helping him. Where had he gone? He remembered Taza saying something but couldn't remember what it was. The bite hurt and the he suddenly felt woozy. Shock. He saw Raven next to him, still trying to back away from the bear, but he had trouble hearing. He turned his head to look for Taza, but his vision began to blur. Where was Taza?

From the ground he caught a glimpse of Taza, just in time to see him fire his gun. The bear collapsed. Even though he knew it had to be dead, he could still hear its snarl—not the angry snarl of before but more like a moan.

Everything seemed to move in slow motion. He watched from a distant place as Taza took out his knife. Why would he do that? Wasn't the bear dead yet?

"Kian! Kian, listen to me."

Kian turned his head, but still had difficulty understanding Taza.

"You're going to be all right, son. Hang in there."

With one swift move the knife cut through the boy's pant leg, up past his knee. Kian felt Taza rotate his leg but couldn't see where the bear had bitten him. He closed his eyes and never saw Taza cut his pant leg into strips and bound his leg above the bite. Surprisingly, he never felt it either. Kian couldn't understand why Taza was holding his leg so tight. He hoped whatever Taza was doing would help stop the pain.

Taza laid Kian down under a small tree and then brought one of the saddlebags over to him and began to bandage up the wound. He had brought the first-aid supplies they needed to patch up a wound, but he didn't have anything to stop the bleeding.

Kian was not completely unconscious. Taza knew he was in shock. When Taza looked into Kian's eyes, the boy returned a blank, hollow stare. Taza knew that he needed to act quickly.

Kian remembered hearing Taza talking the whole time he was wrapping up his leg. He wanted to answer him, but whenever he tried, his lips seemed to be thick—like talking with oatmeal in his mouth. It was impossible to speak. He heard something about Doc Benson and whether he should go get him or bring Kian to the doc.

"If I could just sleep," Kian thought, but voices kept buzzing in his head.

Taza wrapped a horse blanket around Kian, and propped his head with another. He told Kian to stay right there until he got back. Kian tried to answer Taza, but his lips just wouldn't move.

~ ~ ~ ~ ~

Kian wasn't sure how much time passed when he heard what he thought was a car or truck off in the distance. He wasn't sure if he really heard something, or if he was dreaming. When he opened his eyes, he was not familiar with his surroundings. He remembered Taza had left him under a small tree, but now he was wedged between two rocks, and there was no sign of the tree at all.

It seemed like a long time had gone by when Kian finally heard someone yelling. "Kian! Kian, where are you?"

Kian tried to answer but couldn't. Who was shouting? Why couldn't he answer? He closed his eyes. It seemed like a long time before he heard voices again.

"Up here, Doc! He's up here."

Taza found him wedged between two rocks a short distance from the tree. Taza gently picked him up and placed him on a flat area next to the doctor.

"He's alive," Taza said. "He's cold, but breathing."

As the doc rolled up Kian's sleeve, Kian realized that it was him they were talking about. He heard the doc tell Taza to go get the water. That was the last thing he remembered.

~ ~ ~ ~ ~

The first thing Kian noticed was the smell. He hadn't opened his eyes yet, but he could smell cornbread. When he finally did open them, he searched the room, trying to figure out where he was. It looked familiar, but he was having a hard time piecing it all together.

This is my room, he thought, *my bed in my house.* He was at home. But why would he be in bed in the middle of the day? He tried to pull back the covers, but he just didn't have the strength.

"Well, look who finally decided to join us." It was his father. He was carrying a tray with something on it that looked like soup.

"Pop-o." Kian tried to smile, but even that took too much of an effort.

"I don't think you're quite ready to be getting out of bed. Let me help you sit up so you can eat some of this chicken broth."

Kian's father pulled the pillow from the bed and placed it against the headboard, then helped Kian sit up.

"Pop-o, I think I saw the Magic Sunrise."

Kian's father raised his eyebrows. "Really?"

"Grandpa told me all about the Magic Sunrise. He said there were only four days out of the year you could see it, and this wasn't one of them. Then, when we were starting to leave . . ." Kian scratched the top of his head for a moment as he tried to remember what happened next, and then continued, ". . . something hurt my leg. I reached down to grab my leg. There was an explosion. When I looked up, I saw the Magic Sunrise. At least I thought I did, but . . . I couldn't have if today isn't one of the four days."

Kian lowered his eyes, avoiding his father's stare.

"What's the matter, son?"

Kian hesitated. Finally, he said, "After I saw the sunrise, I . . ." he hesitated again. "I . . . well, I saw Mom." Again, Kian paused before he continued. Finally, he went on, his voice louder and more excited. "I mean I really saw her! Not like when I speak with her spirit. It seemed like she was right there . . . But that couldn't be, could it, Pop-o?"

Kian's father set the tray down on Kian's lap and told him to try and eat the broth. "When you're finished, we'll talk about what happened, okay?"

Kian nodded and began to sip the broth.

When Kian's father came back a short time later, Kian had finished the broth and half of the water. He was just beginning to doze off when Pop-o walked in.

"Ready for a little nap?" his father asked.

"I'm a little tired, but can we talk for a while first?"

His father took the tray from Kian's lap and set it on the dresser, then sat down on the chair next to his bed. "So what's on your mind?"

"Well, I'm starting to remember some of what happened . . . I think, but not everything."

Kian's father put the back of his hand on Kian's forehead. "Your fever has finally broken. Looks like you'll be up doing your chores in no time. Let me tell you what I know, and then you can ask questions after that, okay?"

When he had finished telling Kian everything he knew, Pop-o smiled at Kian. "You lost a great deal of blood. It was touch and go for a while, but the doctor says you'll be just fine."

"So, you think it was just a dream, when I saw the Magic Sunrise and . . ." he hesitated for a second, "Mom?"

"I guess it really doesn't matter what I think, does it? What do you think, Kian?"

"It seemed real. She was right in front of me, but it must have been a dream or vision or something like that."

39

Kian pulled the covers up to his chin, then looked into his father's eyes.

His father chose his words carefully. "The way I see it, son, is like this. You can sit and wonder whether it was a dream or a vision or real or whatever, but that isn't going to change anything. Why not just appreciate that you saw your mother, and leave it at that?"

"Mom really was pretty, wasn't she?"

"Your mother was a very beautiful woman, Kian, and a wonderful person. She loved you very much. You do know that, don't you, son?"

"Yes, Pop-o, I know."

"Okay then, you better get some rest now. You need to get your strength back because I'm getting tired of doing all the work around here."

Kian smiled at his father. "Okay, I will." Then he closed his eyes, and in no time he was fast asleep.

Almost a week passed before Kian was well enough to help around the house and do some of his chores but it was hard for him to stay in bed that whole time.

"I'm just fine today," Kian would say, but then he'd get out of bed and feel dizzy and weak. His father would have to tell him to get back in bed and just wait until he had rested enough to gain back his strength.

~ 6 ~

The summer was quickly coming to an end, and Kian wasn't very happy about it. Before long he would have to go back to school. Kian didn't actually dislike school. But he liked summer so much more. He was happy doing chores, and he liked working around the house and fixing things. He was becoming a good carpenter. His neighbor had shown him how to garden and he enjoyed that too. Now that it was getting late into the summer, he was picking vegetables.

He especially liked riding Raven daily. Kian had become an excellent rider and seldom used a saddle. He and Raven had become closer friends, if that was possible. Raven was a strong, fast horse, and also a very smart one. Kian's grandfather told him horses weren't very smart. They followed commands but usually didn't think on their own. Raven was different. He seemed to know just what to do even before Kian gave him a command.

Kian and his father went to the rocky shore of Lake Superior once after Taza had brought him there. When

Kian and his father arrived where the bear had bitten Kian, he was concerned, but his father assured him the chances of a bear being in that same spot were pretty slim. Kian saw Raven remembered the incident also. He didn't want to go by the bush where he'd been tied, so they tied the horses in a different place. Unfortunately, this wasn't a day the Magic Sunrise took place. But Kian liked being there anyway. The beauty of the lake and the crashing waves against the huge, granite rocks was a spectacular sight.

Later that month, Kian asked his father if he could go to Lake Superior by himself. His father was hesitant, but decided Kian was old enough to make the journey alone.

The first time he went there, he had planned to leave Raven at the same place they had left him in the past and climb to the ledge that looked out over the beautiful lake alone. Raven did not particularly like it when Kian tried to tie him and reared up, pulling the reins free from Kian's hands.

Kian looked at Raven and said, "Just what do you think you are doing? Do you think you can go with me?" He stroked Raven's neck and laughed. "Don't you realize the path is too narrow and rocky for someone your size?"

Raven pushed his nose up against Kian's shoulder and nudged him, as if to say, *"Get moving. I'll follow."*

Kian decided to walk up the path a ways to see what Raven would do. Of course, Raven followed. Kian continued, and sure enough, so did Raven. When they got to the last fifteen or twenty feet, the part like climbing up steps, Kian thought Raven would not be able to go further. Raven studied the terrain a moment, then continued. They went slowly and carefully, but the two of them made it to the top. Once there, though, Raven wouldn't go near the edge. He seemed just fine where he was.

Each time Kian visited this sacred place he sat in the middle of the flat ledge that looked out over the lake. This is where Kian liked to sit and speak to his mother's spirit.

Many times, he would close his eyes and see his mother's face staring down at him. He'd remember how his mother used to read to him when he was younger. He could see her sitting in the big stuffed chair in the living room with him on her lap, looking up into her deep-brown eyes as she read. Her hair was long and jet black, and she always smelled so good. When it was time for bed, he'd say, "Will you read just a little more . . . please?" And she would always give in and say, "Oh, all right, just one more page," as she smiled down at him. Afterward, when Kian and Raven made the trip back down the cliffs, the whole way down Kian would feel so good inside because he had seen the magnificent beauty and power of the Great Lake and because he had visited with his mother.

As many times as Kian and Raven went to the Great Lake, they still had not been able to witness the Magic Sunrise. Kian knew when the time of the year for the Magic Sunrise came, there'd be too many things happening for them to go—school for Kian and Pop-o would be trying for as much work as possible before the slow season. Kian was sure his father would not let him travel the rocky cliffs of Lake Superior alone at that time of morning, but he vowed to himself that someday, when the time was right, he too would get to witness the Magic Sunrise.

~ ~ ~ ~ ~

Now that Kian was twelve, he feared very few things. He had ridden his horse bareback at full speed, been bitten by a bear and sat on the edge of a cliff looking over the treacherous rocks and waves of Lake Superior. No, there weren't too many things that frightened him.

The one thing that did, however, was thunderstorms. Kian could not think of a good reason why he disliked thunderstorms, but he did. Maybe it was because the storms almost always had lots of lightning, or maybe it was because he knew his father didn't like them either. It didn't matter. He just didn't like them and didn't think he'd ever get used to them.

Kian was sure Raven felt the same about thunder and lightning. Whenever there was a storm, Kian would go out in the shed and sit with Raven. It seemed to do both of them a lot of good.

One time, in the middle of the night, Kian heard the rumbling of thunder off in the distance. He snuck out to the shed to stay with Raven. He was only going to stay until the storm passed, but he fell asleep. His father found him there the next morning. He told Kian from now on he needed to stay in the house during a storm.

Usually by the end of July most of the severe weather was over. If a storm did come through this late in the summer, it wasn't much of a storm, short-lived, with little rain and very few claps of thunder.

It was late in the evening and just starting to get dark when Kian's father heard bad weather was brewing just west of Duluth and heading northeast. He had seen this kind of storm before and told Kian not to worry. Most of these storms fell apart when they got near the lake since the cooler air over the lake tended to push the storms east instead of north toward them. He was pretty sure it wouldn't be much of anything.

This time turned out to be different. When the storm made it to Lake Superior—just above Duluth—the lake air wasn't cool enough to pull it east. The storm followed the shoreline, heading right over their property. By the time it reached them, it had grown powerful. It hit after midnight, and that only compounded the problem.

Around ten o'clock that evening, Kian heard the rumble of the storm way off in the distance. He went to his father's room and asked if he could go out to the shed to check on Raven and Morton, his father's horse.

"You can go check on them, Kian, but don't stay out there all night like you did the last time."

"Yes, Pop-o," Kian answered, "I'll come back in."

Kian went to Raven and stroked his neck. He could tell Raven was already agitated. The horse threw up his head every time he heard distant thunder. Kian wished he could stay with Raven, but he knew he'd better get back to the house before his father came and got him.

Kian lay in his bed wide awake, listening as the thunder got louder and the lightning flashed brighter the closer the storm got. He knew he'd never get to sleep until the storm passed. He could only hope Raven, his best friend in the whole world, would be all right.

The rain came down in torrents. The wind blew it hard against the south side of the house. Kian heard his father get up and move around in his room. *He must be looking outside to see if the storm has done any damage,* Kian thought. He wanted to see if the shed was still okay, but his bedroom window didn't face that direction.

Through the noise of thunder and beating rain, Kian thought he heard something else. It almost sounded like pounding on the shed. He tried to make out what the sound might be, but the frequent claps of thunder made it impossible to tell. He wondered if it was Raven trying to kick down the door, so he and Morton could run free. He wanted so much to go out and be with them.

Kian thought the pounding had stopped, but all of a sudden a bright flash filled his room. It was so bright Kian had to squint his eyes. At that very same instant came a loud explosion. Together the lightning bolt and thunder threw Kian from his bed. He landed hard. Before he got up his father was standing in his doorway.

"Kian! Kian, are you all right?"

"Yes, Pop-o, I think so. What happened?"

"I'm not sure. A bolt of lightning might have hit close by. You stay here. I'm going out to check."

"But, Pop-o, let me go with—"

"No, Kian! You stay here, do you understand? I'll be right back."

Kian feared the lightning had hit the shed. He wanted to see if the horses were okay. He didn't know how they could be from the sound of the blast, but he needed to find out if anything had happened to Raven.

Kian's heart began to race. All he could think was, *What if the lightning hit the shed? What if something happened to Raven?* He waited until he heard the outside door shut, and then jumped up and raced into his father's room. When he looked out the window, his worst fears were confirmed.

"Noooo! Pop-o, no!" he screamed.

He didn't wait to see if his father turned around and looked. He just took off down the stairs fast. He flew out the back door and ran toward the pile of rubble that used to be the shed, wearing only his underwear. Pop-o stood between him and the shed. Kian almost ran right into him. His father tried to calm Kian, but Kian was frantic.

"Raven! Pop-o, is Raven okay? Please, Pop-o, we have to help Raven."

His father held Kian tightly and looked directly into his eyes. "Listen to me, Kian, listen." He had to shake him in order to get his attention. "Go back to the house. Put some dry clothes on. I'll check the shed and see if the horses are all right. Go in the house and get dressed."

"But, Pop-o, I need to—"

"You need to go into the house and get out of those wet clothes. Do as I said. Do you understand?" Pop-o squeezed Kian's arms just hard enough to hurt, then shook him a little. "Do you understand?"

Kian broke down crying and said, "Yes, Pop-o." He slowly turned and went back to the house. He sat at the kitchen table, watching his father, who was heading toward the pieces of wood that used to be the shed. *There's no way that Raven could be alive under that pile of rubble*, Kian thought.

The storm had not let up. Sheets of rain pounded against Kian's father as he sifted through the pile of wood. Lightning strikes continued. Kian worried for his father's safety. But he needed to know if there was any hope that either of the animals was still alive.

It looked like the lightning must have hit the shed right in the middle, split it in half, because there were actually two piles separated by a small space in the middle.

Kian could see his father still hadn't found the horses. He watched as Pop-o examined both piles once more. *Could they have somehow gotten out before the lightning hit?* Kian wondered.

With the lightning striking more often now, Pop-o didn't feel safe outside anymore. He came in. There wasn't anything he could do out there tonight, anyway.

Kian put his head down on the kitchen table and cried when he saw his father coming in. He cried so hard and so much that there was not only a puddle on the floor from his dripping clothes, but also a puddle of tears on the table. He wasn't sure if he was crying because he was relieved his father hadn't found Raven, or because he was scared Raven could still be harmed by the storm. All he knew for sure was that he wanted Raven back home.

When Kian's father came in, he explained what he had discovered after searching the pile of rubble. "They must have gotten out before the lightning hit. Neither of the horses is there . . . I just don't understand it."

Kian's head bolted up from the table. "Then we have to go find them," he said and headed to the door. When he got there, he looked down and realized all he wore was his wet underwear.

He turned around, and his father was standing there looking down at him. "We will, Kian, but not now. Tomorrow, when the storm has blown over and we have daylight. Then we'll look for them."

"But, Pop-o, they might—" His father held him by the shoulders but didn't say anything. Kian knew it wouldn't do any good to argue. He looked up at him and said, "Okay, Pop-o, tomorrow." He hesitated, then asked, "Will they be all right Pop-o?"

"I hope so, son. I hope so."

Kian lay in bed, looking up at the ceiling, wide awake. He knew he wouldn't be able to sleep. He thought about Raven and Morton and where they might have gone.

Kian knew the horses would try and find shelter, but where? At first, he thought they might go to Mrs. Harris's farm next door. He dismissed that. He remembered she didn't have any shelter for them. Her shed had burned down a few years back, and she had no reason to replace it since she didn't have animals.

Then he thought about how much Raven meant to him and his father. Ever since his father had started to ride Raven again, he had seemed happier and more fun to be with. Kian knew Raven helped his father get through the loss of his mother, and wondered how hard it would be on both of them if they were unable to find Raven.

~ 7 ~

T he next morning Kian and his father were up at the crack of dawn. Kian looked out his bedroom window. The sky was perfectly clear. He saw little evidence of the storm, other than the demolished shed and large puddles. Because most of the soil was either rocky or clay, it took a long time for the rain to soak in. Most of the path that led to the main road was under water. He worried his father would say they couldn't go look for the horses until the water subsided.

Kian was downstairs before his father, dressed and ready. His father didn't try to talk Kian into having breakfast before they left. Instead he put some leftover corn bread in a bag to bring along. Kian only had one thing on his mind—finding Raven.

The storm had washed away any trail the horses' might have left. As they drove down the path to the main road, they talked about where the horses might have sought refuge.

"Do you think they went to the cliffs?" Kian asked.

"That'd be my guess," his father said. "There are good sheltered areas in those caverns. We'll check there."

He drove the truck down a sandy, washed out road that led to the base of Shovels Point—the first of several areas the horses might have gone. The rain had washed away parts of the road, and he had to drive slowly to keep the truck from getting stuck. Kian looked way out in front of the truck in hopes he would see the horses.

"There they are!" Kian yelled and pointed to the right of the truck. "That looks like Morton." He strained his eyes, but couldn't see Raven anywhere. "Where's Raven?" he asked. "I don't see Raven."

"He may still be in one of the caverns. Don't worry, son, we'll find him."

They tied Morton to the bumper of the truck and walked to the caverns on foot. Kian yelled Raven's name as they searched, but no black horse was to be found.

Kian and Pop-o were puzzled. Normally the horses would stick together—unless of course, something happened. But, if something had happened to Raven, they should have seen evidence of it. Maybe Raven and Morton had gone separate ways. Thinking about this, Kian became more and more concerned. When he brought this up, his father said it wasn't likely, "The horses know their chances are better if they stay together."

They spent the rest of the morning searching the caverns. No trace of Raven. Finally, Kian's father said they would bring Morton back to the house, have something to eat, then make a trip the other way toward town. Maybe someone in town had seen him.

That evening, they sat at the supper table in silence. Kian's father had re-heated some of the previous day's stew. Kian was picking at it with his fork, but he hadn't eaten much. His mind was somewhere else.

They spent the next two days searching all the places they believed Raven could have traveled. They also stopped and talked to anyone who might have seen or heard something about him. They even tried some places that they didn't think he could have gone, but they never saw a trace of him. It was like he'd just disappeared. All the searching and asking about Raven produced nothing.

Kian's father had to get back to work and Kian needed to start caring for the farm. The storm had left them a lot of work. His father also had plenty of work since the storm had damaged a number of homes in the area. Kian knew Pop-o could make extra money. They would need it to rebuild the shed.

Kian knew both of them needed to do work to get their minds off of Raven, but he didn't know what might help. Whenever Kian wasn't busy, he thought about Raven. He missed him so much.

Pop-o was working later and leaving earlier in the morning. Kian found himself making his own breakfast and sometimes eating supper by himself. Many times, when

Pop-o did get home, he wanted to be alone. He'd ask Kian about his day, but neither Kian nor Pop-o felt like talking.

Deep in his heart, Kian believed Raven was still alive. If he wasn't, they should have found some trace of him. Kian felt he had to do something, but he just didn't know what. It was tearing him up inside. He hoped that soon he would figure out what it was he should do.

Time dragged. It had only been a short time since Raven disappeared, but to Kian it seemed like forever. He tried to stay busy all the time to keep from wondering about Raven. Other times, he looked at pictures he had gotten from his mother, or read the books she had left him, but many times this made Kian even sadder because he still missed his mother, too.

If Raven was alive somewhere, he couldn't just sit and wait for the horse to come back. Kian needed to figure out where Raven had gone.

He believed the only thing left to do was ask his mother and the Indian spirits to give him direction and guidance to find Raven. They were his last hope. If they couldn't help him, Kian wasn't sure that anybody could.

Kian really hoped that the spirits would be able to help, not just for himself, but for his father, too. He knew his father was becoming depressed, and Kian was afraid he might start drinking again, as he had after Mother died.

He decided the best place to speak with the spirits would be at the cliffs of Lake Superior. This might be his only hope of getting help to find Raven, so he wanted to make sure he did it right. Maybe the spirits would give him a sign of where Raven might be, or advise him what to do.

Kian was pretty sure his father would never allow him to go to the Lake Superior cliffs alone because of how depressed Kian had been lately. He also knew that his father couldn't take him there with all the extra work available from the storm. Besides, he was pretty sure his father wouldn't agree with the idea anyway.

He thought about asking Taza, but the last time they'd spoken, Taza had told Kian it was time for him to move on. He said he should realize some things are just meant to be. "Perhaps it was Raven's time," he said. Kian had cried all night after that. He was beginning to wonder if maybe Taza was right. But Kian also knew he had to at least ask the spirits for their help. He carefully made plans and then waited for the best opportunity to carry them out.

A few days before Kian planned to make his trip to Lake Superior, he woke up very early, went out onto the porch, and looked out at the horizon. Moments later, as he expected, he heard his father's footsteps in the hallway. The back door opened, and his father stepped out on the porch with him. Kian was right. He figured that if he got up in the middle of the night and went downstairs, his father would come down to see what he was doing.

"Are you having trouble sleeping?" Pop-o asked.

"A little, I guess. Sometimes, I just like to come out here and look and see if . . . well, just look."

"I wish there was something I could do to make things better, Kian, but I don't know what. I'm really sorry this happened. It will get better, for both of us. I promise."

Kian just nodded, looking out at the horizon. The skyline was beginning to lighten ever so slightly, which meant the night would soon give way to the morning.

Kian's father turned and went back into the house. As he did he said, "There's still time to get an hour's sleep before sunrise."

Kian went back to his room and lay down. He hoped the next time his father heard him get up in the middle of the night he wouldn't bother checking on him.

He thought about what he needed before he made his trip to the cliffs. He'd get some of the special powder hidden in a box in his father's closet. His father had shown it to him once. He told Kian Taza gave it to his mother. Their ancestors used the powder in some ceremonies. Kian wasn't sure what he was supposed to do with the powder, but he knew that once he got to the lake and started to speak to the spirits, he'd figure it out.

Three days later, Kian decided it was the right time to go to the cliffs. He had taken some of his mother's tribal powder the day before when his father was at work. Two small handfuls were all he figured he'd need.

He awoke as planned about two hours before sunrise, slipped out of bed and picked up the bundle of clothes he'd prepared the night before. He decided to hide his clothes on the porch instead of putting them on. He'd wait a couple of minutes to see if his father got up. If he did, Kian would wait until his father went back upstairs as he had the last time. If his father saw him fully dressed, he'd surely get suspicious and question him.

Kian stood on the porch, hoping his father wouldn't come down. He felt bad enough planning this trip without including his father. He felt as if he were lying to him, but he didn't know any other way. He would make it up to him when this was all over.

After a few minutes, Kian decided it was safe to continue on his journey. He picked up the bundle of clothes, and snuck out to the new shed where he slipped into his shirt and pants, and quietly prepared Morton for the ride to the Great Lake Superior.

The quarter moon cast just enough light for Kian to see. He walked Morton down the path to the main road, to make as little noise as possible. When he looked back, the house was still dark. His father hadn't heard him leave.

Morton had been to the cliffs enough times he pretty much knew the way. Kian just pointed him in the right direction, and Morton did the rest. Kian didn't want to go too fast. It was still dark, and he didn't want Morton getting hurt. Besides, there was plenty of time to get there at a slow easy pace. Kian had planned it that way.

While he rode, Kian wrestled with mixed feelings about the trip. One part of him felt good he was finally doing something that might lead to Raven's return. Another part of him worried that, if he didn't get any information about Raven, he might have to accept that Grandfather had been right: Raven's disappearance was meant to be and he'd never see Raven again. He didn't like thinking about that.

Finally, Kian considered the biggest problem with this trip, about what he was doing to his relationship with his father. He loved Pop-o, and he knew how much his father loved and trusted him. He knew this would hurt him. That bothered Kian a lot. He thought about returning home, but he also knew this was his last hope of finding Raven. He just had to go through with it.

He reached the place he would leave Morton. As soon as Kian dismounted, Morton began to munch on the sparse grass that grew between the rocks.

Kian removed the saddlebag and tied Morton to an overgrown alder next to the trail. He began to climb the narrow path that led to the top—the last leg of his journey. All he could think about was finding Raven.

When he reached the top, he looked out over the edge of the cliff, but it was too dark to see anything. He could hear the crashing of the waves against the huge boulders. The eastern skyline just began to be lighter than the west. *It's at least a half an hour until sunrise,* Kian thought. He sat down next to the saddlebag, wondering if his father had found the note he had left.

Kian looked to the east and realized it was closer to sunrise than he'd first thought. He had forgotten the eastern cliffs hid the sunrise, so he wouldn't know exactly when it came. Looking at the sky, Kian felt it was time—time to ask the spirits for their help.

He took out the pouch of special powder and set it on a rock. He took out the picture of his mother and her necklace his father had given to him shortly after she died. He opened the pouch and poured the powder in one of his hands, then set the pouch down and divided the powder between both hands. He took a long, hard look at his mother's picture, wishing she was here to advise him.

He stood and walked over to the large, flat rock that stuck out from the edge of the cliff. Standing at its edge, he looked at the beautiful sunrise and listened to the rhythm of the waves hitting the rocks below. Seeing the mighty lake and all its power, he knew if there ever was a time to speak to the spirits and ask for help, it was now.

With his hands at his sides, he closed his eyes, and thought about Raven. Then he said in a loud voice, "Oh, spirits from my past, if it is in your power to help me find Raven, speak to me. Tell me what to do."

In one quick motion he threw his arms above his head, jumping straight into the air releasing the powder high into the sky, and then he came down hard and landed on the rock. *CRAAACK!* Kian immediately felt the rock giving way beneath his feet.

Kian's eyes became as large as saucers and his arms and legs trembled. Fear seized him. He scrambled desperately for the edge, but gravity won, and he began the frightful fall to the angry waves below. He knew he could do nothing. He closed his eyes, and tumbled through the air, accepting what had happened.

The cool morning air rushed against his body, and blew through his hair as he fell. For some strange reason everything seemed to be going in slow motion. The fear Kian felt when the rock first broke left him. He couldn't understand why, but he felt at ease. He knew he was falling to the rocks and water below, but a calm engulfed him, and he believed that everything would be all right.

With his eyes still shut, Kian felt the need to spread out his arms like a bird spread its wings. The tumbling stopped, and he felt the rushing wind against his body change. Now a gentle wind was pushing against his face and his chest. It came not from underneath him, but from in front of him. He felt he was no longer dropping, but more like he was . . . like he was flying alongside the cliff wall. How could that be?

He wanted to open his eyes but was afraid. None of this made sense. By now he should have crashed against the boulders in Lake Superior, yet he hadn't. Stranger yet, he seemed to be . . . flying. *Maybe I'm dreaming*, he thought. Kian realized the only way he'd know would be if he opened his eyes. So he did.

The first thing he noticed was the lake and rocks were still a long way down. He had probably only dropped half way to the bottom. Next, he realized he no longer was dropping, he was gliding next to the cliff wall, just as he had imagined. Suddenly it hit him. He understood why he hadn't dropped to the rocks, why he was gliding along the walls of the cliffs—he was flying. Somehow, he had been transformed into a bird—a large, black bird—either a crow or a raven.

As he soared, next to the cliffs, he tilted his head down to the left, then instinctively lifted his right wing. Immediately he glided down to the left. After dropping fifty feet he brought the wing level again. Once again he soared parallel to the raging waves below. He never had to think about what to do next. Everything came naturally.

Kian realized that, even though he had the instincts and body of a bird, he still had his own mind, his own thoughts. This was more than he could comprehend. He saw a dead birch sticking out between two rocks high up on the cliff. Dropping his right wing, he flew directly toward it. Seconds before he would have crashed into the cliff, he lifted his head, turned his wings inward, flapped them rapidly backward. He slowed enough to grasp the birch branch with his claws. Just like that, he was perched atop the snag.

In one quick motion, he jumped in the air, turned his body, and landed on the same branch so he could look down at the lake below. Kian examined his new body, lifting each wing and inspecting it. He turned his head as far around as possible, looking at his tail feathers and his back. He was definitely a bird. He had a long, sleek, black, shiny body. When he extended his wings, each one was at least the length of his body. Kian thought this was why he was able to soar so well. Kian realized he was a raven. And as he was inspecting himself, he was also instinctively checking his surroundings, making sure no predator or danger lurked nearby.

What happened? Kian thought. *Have the spirits somehow changed me into a bird. Am I dreaming? And if this isn't a dream and I really am a bird, why do I think like a boy?* Just thinking about all of this frustrated him. A part of him wanted to take off and fly, just fly.

He remembered sitting on his porch back home, watching hawks and ravens high in the sky, soaring in big circles. He remembered wishing he could join them. Now he could do that if he wanted to. But something held him back. Something didn't feel right. Was it the bird instinct in him that kept him on his perch? For some reason this didn't seem like the time to be soaring.

Another part of him wanted to go home. Already he missed Pop-o and Taza. Would he ever get to see them again? And if he did, would it be through the eyes of a bird or a boy? This whole ordeal was very confusing. He wanted to shout, *"AM I A BIRD OR A BOY?"* but he couldn't. Kian also believed one reason he had been changed into a bird was so he could look for Raven. Kian spent much of that day just sitting on the dead birch stump, wondering about his fate as a bird and wrestling with the fact that he had the mind of a boy.

That afternoon Kian realized he needed a place to spend his first night as a bird. Predators hunted during the night. He needed somewhere safe to stay. After carefully surveying the area, he realized that his birch perch was safe. He was quite sure only a bird could get to it.

The following morning, Kian flew around the area, making sure it would be a safe place to stay until he figured out just exactly what he was going to do. More important, he needed to find food. By noon Kian had checked the area thoroughly and decided he'd stay here for now.

It didn't take him long to realize he needed to eat. He was hungry but wasn't sure what he would eat. Kian realized it wasn't the same as when he was at home. As a boy, when he got hungry, he ate. It was as simple as that because the food was right there. As a bird it was different. He needed to search for food. If he didn't find any, he would go hungry. He was concerned because, if he hadn't found any food before nightfall, he'd have to wait until the next day. A raven wasn't one of those predators that could hunt at night.

Kian got lucky. While he was flying above some pine trees, not far from the top of the cliffs, he noticed a small patch of alder bushes with something entangled in them. He saw it was a half-eaten rabbit left there by some other animal. He landed in the bush and looked at the rabbit carcass in disgust. Whatever animal had caught this poor rabbit tore it into pieces. Its head was the only part that looked like it hadn't been touched. Both of its hind legs were completely missing and one of the front legs was only half there. Some of its insides were on the ground below its body. The flies had deposited their eggs in several places in the rabbit's stomach cavity, and already they were turning into maggots.

Kian's first reaction was to fly away and find something else, but the raven instinct took over. Kian flew down to the rabbit and began searching through the carcass for something still worth eating. The feeling of disgust left him, and he had no problem picking through the carcass. He ate until full. The insects would take care of the rest.

Kian left the rabbit and flew high into the air above the trees and then over the cliffs and the lake. He flew next to the granite cliffs, examining the different rock formations, then dropped low barely above the water. The water was so deep and dark that even with the bright sunlight it was impossible to see any depth. He realized if he hadn't been changed into a bird, his body would never be found once it hit the rocks and floated away.

Back up to the top of the cliffs, he noticed movement where the rock had broken off. He wasn't exactly sure what it was, but it looked like someone peering down into the lake below. He dropped his right wing and made a large swooping turn in hopes of getting a better look. He was overcome by familiarity but wasn't sure why.

He brought his right wing back up and started to fly toward the broken rock. When he was able to see the opening again, nobody was there. Had he imagined the movement, or had someone been there? Was it his father?

He flew back to his resting place—the dead birch branch. This was a place he felt comfortable, but he wasn't sure why. He was pretty sure the bird instinct liked this place because it was safe. The boy part of him liked it as well, because it overlooked the Lake Superior and the beautiful rock formations to the east. In the morning, the sun splashed brilliant colors against the huge jagged rocks making for a spectacular sunrise.

While Kian was perched on the branch he noticed small pieces of meat and blood on his legs and his breast feathers, probably from the rabbit. What would his father have said if he had eaten like this at home? He spent the next ten minutes cleaning and preening his feathers.

Looking out into Lake Superior, Kian noticed an island a short distance to the north. He jumped off the branch and soared down toward the water, then turned his head upwards and pumped his wings hard several times. Soon he was high above the cliffs—so high the small island looked like a dot in the water. When he reached an altitude that seemed like miles above everything, he stretched his wings straight out and tipped his head a little. His body leveled out so he could soar. He made big circles above the lake and cliffs, never losing altitude. At this altitude the air was much cooler—in fact, almost cold.

The cliffs appeared nothing more than a shoreline. He could see a long ways down the coast of Lake Superior and wondered what it'd be like exploring the entire shoreline. The boy in him wanted to leave right away. *It'd be a very interesting adventure,* he thought. The more he thought about it the more he wanted to go.

At the same time this idea worked through one part of his mind, the other part (the bird part) told him to stay. Ravens liked familiar territories. Kian did not like the struggle going on in his mind. Why couldn't he just make a decision and do something if he wanted? The more he wrestled, the more he felt he should listen to the bird part of his mind, at least for now. In the back of his mind, he knew the real reason he wasn't making any moves right away. He knew he still needed to figure out what, if anything, he was going to do about finding his best friend in the whole world, Raven.

On the way back down to his perch, Kian decided to play. At first he pretended he was a dive-bomber and dove straight to the bottom of the cliffs. He flew so fast the wind made his eyes water. Only a few feet from the water, he turned sharply, quickly flying parallel to the lake.

He flew in and out of the jagged rocks along the cliffs. He kept looking for smaller and narrower crevices to challenge himself. Some were so narrow he had to tilt his wings and fly sideways to keep from hitting the sides.

Finally, Kian flew back to his perch to rest. He could feel his heart pound and realized he had actually had fun. He'd been playing like he used to back home. He wondered if other birds (ones that didn't have the mind of a boy) played like that, or was what they did for survival only.

The sun was just beginning to drop below the trees in the west, and it blanketed the whole sky with shades of crimson red and purple. *It's beautiful*, Kian thought. *I wish Pop-o and Taza were here to see it.*

Thinking about sharing this moment with his father and grandfather made him sad. He imagined Pop-o sitting at home by himself, wondering what had become of his son. How had he gotten here in the first place? He got angry, angry with himself. *Why didn't I just accept that Raven was gone? Why did I go to the cliffs alone?* If only he could turn back time and be with his father. Kian spread his wings and tipped his head way back, looked up to the sky, then opened his big black beak and made a loud screeching sound—*Caaaaw! Caaaaaw!*

~ ~ ~ ~ ~

The next morning, Kian realized he was hungry . . . really hungry. All that flying the day before must have taken a lot out of him. He thought about the rabbit but decided he needed something better than the slim pickings of an old, dead rabbit. He wanted something fresh and good.

Kian flew over the tall pine trees a short distance from the lake, and down to the farmland where smaller trees and bushes grew. He had seen small birds there yesterday and hadn't thought too much of it. Now he realized those birds needed to nest somewhere. If he could find a nest, and it had eggs, he could have eggs for breakfast.

He knew he'd need to be sneaky and patient. He sat in one of the tall pines adjacent to the smaller trees and bushes—waiting and watching. He saw a male wood thrush flying from one bush to another, trying to catch an insect.

The wood thrush snatched a butterfly mid-air and then flew to one of the trees and disappeared. Soon the wood thrush was back looking for another insect. After he did this several times, Kian was sure a nest must be in that tree. He was pretty sure the nest had eggs in it and not baby birds because the female wood thrush would also be looking for insects if she had chicks. The male wood thrush was bringing her food. Kian felt lucky to find a late brood.

Kian carefully planned how he'd steal the eggs. He knew that, once the thrushes saw him, they'd do everything in their power to keep him from going near the eggs. Kian hoped several were in the nest. If he took two eggs and there were more, only the male would be able to chase him. The female would need to stay and guard the remaining eggs. Kian would only have to contend with one screeching, pecking, angry bird.

The next time the male snatched an insect to bring to the female, Kian made his move. He jumped off the rock and headed straight for the tree, hoping to catch the two birds off guard. He landed on a branch just above where he had seen the male wood thrush fly into the tree. When he looked down, he saw the female and her nest. As he suspected, as soon as he landed both birds tried to keep him away from their eggs.

The female flew to a branch opposite where the male was perched. That way Kian had to look back and forth to see what each bird was doing. The female jumped from branch to branch, flapping her wings and screeching, trying to get Kian to fly away or come after her. The male stayed near the nest. Each time Kian turned to look at the male and the nest, the female came closer and screeched louder. She hoped Kian would eventually chase her and not go after her eggs, but Kian was not interested in her—he was hungry for eggs.

Kian made his move. He was in luck. The nest held four eggs. Kian jumped off his perch and almost landed on top of the male wood thrush before it moved. The male only moved a short distance realizing Kian was going to steal the eggs. Immediately, the male took to the air and dove at Kian's head, striking him just above his eye.

Kian felt a sharp pain and was glad the bird had not hit his eye. He knew he needed to move quickly. He saw the female flying toward him and put up his wing just as she tried to peck at his other eye. She missed. With one hard flip of his wing, Kian sent the female into a branch but not hard enough to hurt her. In one quick move Kian stabbed his large beak into one of the eggs, sucking out its contents as best he could. Before he could lift his head the male wood thrush flew at him again, this time flapping his wings in the opposite direction as if to land. He struck twice at Kian before he dropped and had to make another pass.

The little birds were smart. They were aiming for Kian's eyes, knowing that was the only place they could do damage to the larger bird. Both thrush came at him at the same time, which made it harder for Kian to eat the egg. He sucked out as much of the first egg as he could, then grabbed one of the other eggs and left. He held up both of his wings just as the two birds tried once again to peck out his eyes. This time he batted at them, which gave him just enough time to take to the air, with both of the birds right alongside him, pecking as Kian tried to pick up speed. He knew the birds were better at maneuvering through the trees than he was, so Kian wanted to get above the trees before they could do any real damage.

Once away from the trees, Kian flew almost straight up, trying to gain as much altitude as possible. The higher he got, the better chance he'd have to ditch the thrush. A short distance from the trees, the female turned back to the nest. The male continued to fly over Kian and dive down at his head.

The male struck twice before Kian finally picked up speed and put enough distance between them that Kian needn't worry. He looked back and noticed the gap between them was getting wider. Even though the wood thrush had no chance of catching up, he continued to follow, probably hoping Kian might drop the egg.

Kian flew high into the sky, holding the egg carefully not to drop or squash it. He wanted to bring the tasty treat back to his spot by the lake, just in case the little bird was waiting for him to come back down.

Finally, Kian went back to the dead birch stub and sat on a rock nearby, inspecting the aqua blue egg. Now that he wasn't being threatened, he had time to think, and the boy in him felt bad for the thrush. It made him think of his father and how sad he must be because, like the two birds, his father had lost someone he loved.

As quickly as the thought occurred, the bird instinct pushed it away. Kian remembered how hungry he was and how good the first egg had tasted. When he looked at the egg, he no longer thought about its pretty blue color, or how the adult thrush must feel. He just thought how good the egg would be inside his stomach. He gently pecked on the egg, hoping to make a big enough hole for his beak to go in but not so big that the insides would run out on the rock. He wanted to savor every last drop of his precious find.

After his meal, Kian cleaned up. He sat on a limb preening, trying to get all of the sticky egg yolk off of his beak and feathers and then combing through his wing feathers with his beak.

As darkness began to turn the lake an inky black and washed the shadows from the cliffs, Kian thought about the day and how much fun he'd had flying through the cliff's crevices and dive-bombing toward Lake Superior. He also thought about the meal he'd had. He felt bad for the little birds, but that feeling went away as he carried out his plan. The bird in him knew he needed to eat in order to survive, so it was okay to take the eggs.

Kian began to realize the rest of his life might be like this. It didn't make him very happy. Even though flying was fun, something was missing. Kian knew what it was—Kian, the boy was lonely. He missed his father and his grandfather and of course, he missed Raven. He wanted to cry, but he couldn't. Birds couldn't cry.

After sitting on his perch and thinking a long, long time, Kian decided what he would do. Tomorrow he would go to the place where the rock broke off and see if he could speak to the spirits. He didn't know if the spirits would listen to a bird, but he knew he had to do something. He wanted his life as a boy back more than anything and he knew that if he had any chance of getting it back, the spirits would be the ones to help him.

The next morning, while soaring high above Lake Superior, Kian spotted the place he was sure was the place where he'd spoken to the spirits. He dropped to have a closer look and circled the area a few times, looking at the edge where the rock broke off. *This has to be the place*, he thought, and he landed on the edge of the broken cliff. Kian realized he remembered some things more easily than others.

As he stood on the edge, looking out over the Great Lake, the place became familiar. Sure this was the place he had visited with his grandfather, he thought of his grandfather. He immediately looked out to the end of the peninsula and saw the arch off in the distance. There was something special about the arch but he wasn't sure what it was. Kian hoped that sooner or later all of his memories would return.

He stretched out his wings and looked up into the sky. He wanted to speak to the spirits, to ask them to change him back to a boy, but no matter how hard he tried, he couldn't because birds can't speak. Kian became frustrated. *There's nothing left to do,* he thought. He decided if the spirits were ever going to change him back to a boy, they'd do it when it was the right time. Maybe the spirits had other plans for him. And maybe the spirits felt it was best for him to remain a bird. They must have made him a bird for a reason, he just didn't know why.

What he did know was he wanted to see his father again and get him to understand everything was all right. He realized how much pain his father must be feeling— losing a son—and hoped his father wouldn't go back to drinking as he did when Kian's mother died.

Kian also thought about Raven. If Raven was still alive, and if Kian could somehow get him back to their farm, maybe his father wouldn't be so lonely. He just wanted Pop-o to be okay.

If Raven was still alive, where was he? Although Kian feared for the worst, he knew that, until he knew for sure Raven was not alive, he'd never truly rest. Raven had been his best friend in the whole world, and Kian knew he couldn't just give up on him.

Kian also realized that, even if he did find Raven alive, he wouldn't be able to speak to him. Kian remembered having special powers that made him able to communicate with some animals, but for some reason he'd never been able to communicate with Raven. But that didn't matter now. The only thing that mattered now was finding Raven.

~ 9 ~

fter watching a magnificent sunrise, Kian set off to find the farm and see his father. Once again, his instincts took over—this time as a boy—and he flew over the point on the cliffs where the rock had broken off. He saw the path that led down the other side of the cliffs and realized he could follow it home.

Kian stayed high. Gliding took a lot less energy than flapping. He hoped he could glide the entire way. He kept a keen watch below, hoping to see his next meal.

The flight took less than half an hour. As he approached the farm and saw the house and shed, he began to experience feelings from the boy in him. He missed the farm, missed the house and the dinners at the kitchen table with his father. He missed the long talks they used to have out on the back porch. He had no idea how hard it would be to visit this place.

He perched on the roof of the porch, then looked out at the shed. The door stood wide open. He could see inside, see movement. Right away his heart began to race.

Could it be Raven? But as quickly as the feeling came, it vanished. That must be Morton, his father's horse.

He stretched out his wings, ready to fly to the shed and see if he was mistaken, but then saw the white markings around the horse's ankle. Raven had no white on his ankles. This wasn't Raven. He wondered if it was a mistake trying to see his father and trying to find Raven.

His father was probably working and wouldn't be home until late, so he perched on the roof, waiting. In the early afternoon, he decided to look for food and see what the rest of the farm was like. He noticed a few places in the fence line that needed repair. When he had taken care of this place those fence lines were fixed daily. Kian could only imagine his father just didn't have the time to work all day and then maintain the farm. This only made him feel worse and more worried about his father.

He passed over Mrs. Harris's garden. Something had knocked over a couple stalks of corn. Two of the ears were exposed. *This corn would make an excellent meal*, he thought, and dove toward it. He landed on the top rail of the fence and looked around to make sure it was safe.

Mrs. Harris was a widow and a very nice lady. Kian liked her a lot. She must have been in the house. Kian was hungry and wanted to start ripping into the corn but the boy in him knew the corn belonged to Mrs. Harris. His bird instinct and his hunger were greater, so he flew over to the corn and feasted. *After all*, he thought, *I am a bird and not a boy anymore.*

In late afternoon he waited on the porch roof, this time looking out toward the tall pines in the far west. He noticed a dot, off in the horizon, next to the pine trees, with a cloud of dust following it. He knew right away it was the truck his father drove to and from work. Within minutes, Kian's father would arrive, and the boy in him became excited. He decided the best place to be when his father arrived was on top of the shed. He could see everything from up there. He jumped off the porch roof, flapped his long slender wings twice, and then glided.

Kian's father drove up the road and stopped next to the shed. Kian watched and waited, but it was a long time before the truck door opened. When Pop-o finally got out, Kian's heart raced. He wanted to fly over to him, to land on his shoulder. Bird instinct knew better. He just watched.

Kian's father stood next to the truck a moment, looking at the shed. For a few seconds Kian thought Pop-o was looking at him. His heart raced even more, wondering if his father recognized him, but then he realized he was looking at the shed door. Pop-o walked over and shut it. He hadn't noticed Kian on the roof at all.

Kian's father finally went into the house. Kian flew to the porch rail and looked in the window. For a long time he saw no one in the kitchen. Pop-o must have gone upstairs. Finally, he heard footsteps on the stairs. Kian watched his father as he moved about the kitchen. His father seemed older now, much older. More streaks of gray marked his hair and more lines mar his face then he remembered. And his father no longer stood up tall and proud like he did when Kian was little.

Kian wondered if his father still kept a bottle in the shed. When Kian's mother had died, Kian found the bottle in the shed. He was too little to do anything about it, but after that day, Kian always wondered if his father was having a drink when he went out to the shed alone.

When his father got to the kitchen, he hesitated, then went to the pantry. Kian thought he was going to get something for his supper. But Pop-o came out of the pantry and set a bottle on the table, then went to the sink for a glass. He no longer kept the bottle in the shed. He kept it right in the kitchen where he could get at it easily. He had no reason to hide it. No one was there to hide it from.

That was all that Kian could take. He flapped his wings and took off for Mrs. Harris's roof. He knew it wouldn't be smart for him to watch his father drink. As he was flying over the garden, thoughts of his father and his past life as a boy began to fade. The instincts of a bird took hold. He needed to find a safe place to stay the night.

Kian woke the next morning in a white pine not far from Mrs. Harris's property line. Instinct had told him that if he stayed there, early in the morning the ground squirrels would be out searching for food and it might be a good place to find his own food. He hoped one of the animals would get far enough from its hole that he could swoop down and grab it before it could make it back.

While he was waiting he thought about how he used to communicate with the chipmunks as a boy. Back then, Kian had thought of them as his friends. Once again, Kian began to wrestle with emotions. How could he be sitting here in this tree waiting for one of those innocent creatures to come out so he could pounce on it and eat it? Weren't they still his friends?

While he struggled with this, he noticed three had come out of their holes and moved around cautiously. His feelings quickly changed. Bird instinct took over. He kept his eye on the smallest one, which didn't appear to be paying much attention to its surroundings. The two larger ones stayed pretty close to one of the holes. If they moved away to find food, they always brought it back near the hole before they ate it. But the smaller one wandered further and further from the safety of the holes. Soon, the time came Kian believed the little rodent was far enough away from its hole that he could catch it before it could get back.

He dropped off the tree branch and spread his wings. The little ground squirrel immediately saw him and took off for the hole. The race was on. Kian knew enough to fly toward the hole, not toward the gopher, since the distance to the hole was closer. When the gopher realized Kian would get to the hole before he could, it turned and headed the other way toward some rocks. That's exactly what Kian wanted. Now he had to grab the little critter before it got to the rocks.

Kian dropped his right wing, turned his head, and then pumped both wings hard to pick up speed. With just two hard flaps Kian was behind it. He stretched out his legs and with one quick motion dropped onto the little gopher just as it was about to jump into the pile of rocks. Then Kian grabbed it with his heavy beak and took it back to the tree to enjoy his meal.

Kian didn't enjoy the meal as much as he thought he would. It wasn't that he didn't like the meat. He loved it. The problem was, the whole time Kian was pulling it apart and devouring the meat, he couldn't help but think about the little chipmunks he used to play with as a boy. How could he eat what could have been one of his playmates? Then he realized, *I'm not a boy. I'm a raven, and ravens don't play with gophers, they eat them.*

The meal barely filled him, but Kian was satisfied, so he let the carcass drop from the tree. He spent the next fifteen minutes cleaning up and preening his feathers. When he had finished, he tried to decide what to do next.

Kian began to realize his life as a raven was not the same as other ravens. Others never had to think about what to do next. Everything they did was instinctive. If he was just a raven with a raven's brain and instincts, it would be easy. He'd just sit in the tree for most of the day until it was time for his next meal. If he became hungry and gophers didn't re-appear, he'd find another food source. If predators such as a hawk came around, he'd find sanctuary in the hills or somewhere. And he knew if he wasn't quick enough and smart enough, he just might become someone else's dinner.

But, when Kian wasn't busy being a bird, he was thinking like a boy—a boy who needed to know about his father and his grandfather and his best friend, Raven. He needed to know if Raven was alive. Even though Kian was a bird, the boy in him kept his thoughts on his past.

After thinking about his next move, he decided he would pay a visit to Taza. He wasn't exactly sure why, since Taza, unlike his father, would, more than likely, be doing fine. He was sure Taza missed him as much as his father did, but he also knew Taza would be able to deal with his departure better. It just seemed right he should see Taza before he went on this journey to find Raven.

Once again, Kian went to a very high altitude and soared rather than flew to his grandfather's place. It wasn't far, so he was there before noon. When he got there, he stayed high above the property, circled it several times before he decided to take a closer look.

Taza's truck was parked next to the porch, and his horse was out in the back of the shed under the lean-to, so Kian was pretty sure that Taza was there. He figured Taza must be busy inside. He finally decided to land on the shed and wait for him there.

After Kian waited a long while on the shed roof, the back door finally opened. Taza came out. He was shirtless and wearing a straw hat when he jumped off the last step of the porch, heading straight for the shed. He appeared to be on a mission. Kian was on the backside of the roof with only his head sticking up, so he was pretty sure Taza wouldn't notice him. He didn't. He went into the shed and came out with an ax. Apparently Taza was going to chop firewood.

The pile of wood was on the other side of the house, so Kian couldn't watch Taza from where he was perched. He'd either need to fly over to the fence line on the other side of the house or sit on top of the house and look down at him. He was less likely to be spotted on the roof, so he went there.

He watched as Taza split wood. It was hard work, especially for someone Taza's age. Kian admired his grandfather, knowing how old he actually was and proud he was able to chop the wood like a thirty-year-old. Kian had always thought that, because his grandfather was in such good shape, he would live forever.

Kian hoped that Taza was checking up on Pop-o regularly. He knew the two of them were close—at least, they were before the accident. Kian hoped his father wouldn't shut Taza out because Pop-o would need Taza to help him get through this.

After fifteen minutes of continuous splitting, Taza finally stopped to rest. He took out his hankie and wiped his brow. When he turned his face away from the hot sun, he looked up at the roof. Kian realized his grandfather must have spotted him. At first he thought nothing of it but then, after a moment, when he realized Taza was still watching him, Kian wondered what his grandfather was thinking.

Taza set down the ax and squinted at the raven more closely. "Are you lost, or just looking for something?" Taza said, softly, but loud enough for Kian to hear.

The bird part of Kian became nervous, and he walked up and down the roofline, watching Taza the whole time. After a few minutes, Kian began to wonder if there was any way Taza might know who he was. He dismissed this crazy notion, realizing it was impossible. Still, the way his grandfather was staring made him a bit uncomfortable.

"You're looking for something, aren't you? Otherwise you would have become too nervous and flown away."

When he said this, a part of Kian wanted to get out of there, but part of him wanted to stay and hear what else Taza had to say. He walked up and down the roofline some more, only this time a little faster.

Taza continued to look at Kian in a strange way. Kian figured Taza must have thought it odd a raven wouldn't fly away under these conditions. Something about the way Taza watched him made him think Taza wanted him to stay and not fly away.

Taza moved to the porch where Kian could no longer see him. After a couple of minutes, Kian flew down to the fence that faced the porch. Once again, he walked nervously up and down the rail, watching Taza the whole time.

For the next few minutes, Taza stood there, looking long and hard at him. When Kian didn't leave, Taza stood up and walked toward the fence. Kian walked further down the fence but didn't fly away. When Taza got to the fence, Kian was still standing on the rail looking at him. He was only twenty feet away. Taza leaned his back against the fence post, then lifted his leg and placed the heel of his boot on the cross board. He stayed in this position for a few moments, then turned and faced Kian once again.

"I'm not exactly sure why you're here or what you want, but for some reason, I have the feeling it might have to do with my grandson. My grandson had special powers. He could communicate with birds and animals. That's the only reason I can think of for you to act like this. If that isn't true, take off and leave right now, but if it is true, well, just stand there on that fence and listen to what I have to say."

This must be strange for Taza, Kian thought. He was pretty sure Taza had never talked to birds before.

"I'm going to tell you what happened to my grandson, Kian, and to his horse, Raven. I know that sounds strange because it sounds strange to me as I'm saying it. If at any time you've had enough, or you think I'm crazy to be talking to a bird, feel free to leave.

"Maybe this is the dumbest thing I've ever done, talking to a bird, or maybe it will do me some good. I don't know. I do know I feel like telling someone this story and as long as you're willing to listen . . . well here goes."

Taza told the bird about Kian and his horse and how close they had become. He talked about the storm and how they never were able to find Raven and how hard that was on Kian. He told him what they thought had happened to Kian and where Raven might have gone. He finished by telling him how hard this was for Kian's father.

"They never found the boy's body, but then, they wouldn't if he did fall off that cliff into the cold deep water of Lake Superior. I'm sure that's why the boy's father is having such a hard time."

Taza stood up straight, turned toward the fence and grabbed the top rail to stretch his back. Kian jumped back a couple of steps, but still didn't fly away.

Looking at the fence, Taza said, "If you're sent by the spirits to help, see if you can find Raven and get him to come back. I don't know why, but I have a feeling he's still alive. If he did come back, I think it would help Kian's father deal with his losses. I just have no idea where that horse could be. Oh, and if you do happen to find out anything about Kian . . ." At the sound of his name, bird-Kian jumped in the air and nodded before landing back on the fence. "Easy there, Mr. Blackbird, I'm not saying you had anything to do with Kian's disappearance. I'm just saying any information about Kian would also be helpful."

Taza turned around and headed back to the woodpile. He shook his head. Kian heard him say under his breath, "I must be going crazy . . . talking to a bird."

Then he hollered over his shoulder, "If you're here to mooch a free meal, there's some corn on the other side of the shed."

Kian silently jumped off the fence and took to the air. He flew almost straight up to a very high altitude, and circled. When he looked back down, Kian noticed Taza was standing by the wood pile, one hand shading his eyes, looking up at him.

Kian knew that his visit there was over. He also knew what he had to do next. He had to find Raven. If there was anything to help Kian's father quit drinking, and get back to a normal life again, it might be the return of Raven.

~ 10 ~

Kian went to a very high altitude once again, this time to conserve energy for what could be a rather long journey. He decided to fly to the cliff above Lake Superior where it all started and make his plans from there. It was the place of the Magic Sunrise, the place where he went to visit the spirit of his mother. It was also the place he went to ask the spirits of his ancestors to help him find Raven. And, of course, it was also the place where Kian the boy became a bird. He believed this should be the place he started his journey to find Raven.

Although Kian had remembered a number of things on his own, it was good to hear Taza tell the story. Kian remembered most of his past. He remembered the good times with his mother before she died and how much fun his father used to be. He also remembered how he used to spend so much time with Raven. But, he didn't remember everything. The part that Kian had the most trouble remembering was when Raven ran away. He was glad that Taza had filled him in.

Kian also worried if, because he was a bird, he might sooner or later lose all of his boy memories. Considering this, Kian knew whatever he was going to do to find Raven, he had better do it quickly.

He spent the night in a small cedar tree overlooking the cliff where Taza had spoken of the Magic Sunrise and where Kian the boy had fallen. He had trouble understanding this concept of being both a bird and a boy and decided he would try to figure it out—not now, though. In the morning he would begin his journey to find Raven.

Kian awoke before sunrise and waited for enough light to head north, on a trail that followed the lake's shoreline. Even though he remembered going that way with his father looking for Raven, he had decided on that direction because of some things Taza had told him. Although Taza hadn't specifically said it would have been very difficult for Raven to travel north along that trail, something in the back of Kian's mind made him think it might have been the way Raven went. Kian could only make decisions based on instinct, and instinct told him to follow the shoreline north.

Heavy fog made it difficult to tell exactly when sunrise arrived. The fog melted into a rather cloudy sky. Kian began to understand why the Magic Sunrise must have been so special to Taza since it not only occurred just four days out of the year, but in Northern Minnesota—especially by Lake Superior—there were many cloudy, foggy mornings. He stretched his wings and preened his feathers then took off for the shoreline trail, flying low enough to see if the horse's carcass was hidden near any of the more deserted trails that led to the lake from the main trail. He also wanted to fly low enough to spot food.

After an hour of flying above the main trail and checking all the trails that led to the lake, Kian thought Raven could have veered from the shoreline trail and headed northwest, following the Temperance River toward the logging camps. Taza had told him he thought Raven might have headed that way because, if he had continued along the shoreline, eventually he would have come to a town and someone would have seen him.

Flying close to the river he glanced from side to side, looking for any openings the horse might have gone for shelter. The river ran wide then narrow with rapids and Kian wondered if Raven would have been able to follow it. Kian spotted a baby rabbit in a clearing not far from the river and flew into an oak tree, hoping the rabbit wouldn't see him. He noticed the mother rabbit not far from the baby but wasn't concerned because he knew if he caught the baby, the mother wasn't a threat. Before Kian even left the tree the mother rabbit sensed trouble and ran toward her den—the baby rabbit close behind—making it safely.

Kian found himself struggling again with his boy emotions and his instincts as a bird. He wanted to find Raven and didn't really care about a stupid baby rabbit for dinner, but the bird part of him knew he needed food in order to survive.

He continued to follow the river, looking for any sign of Raven and searching for food. He spotted the large carcass of what must have been a deer at one time, but when he flew close to it he could tell that it had been killed a long time ago and wasn't worth picking through. He was just beginning to think he wasn't going to have much luck finding a meal when he saw a young muskrat up ahead. He hoped it wouldn't see him until it was too late.

Kian kept one eye glued to the critter as he soared closer. Just as Kian was dropping down to grab it, the muskrat saw Kian, turned and ran for the water. When the muskrat jumped from the rock, trying to reach the water, Kian snatched it in mid-air in his heavy beak and squeezed. Within seconds the muskrat went limp. It was just big enough to make a tasty lunch. Kian found a flat rock somewhat protected from view. He knew if a hawk or a bigger bird came along, it would surely steal his meal. He quickly ripped off each leg and devoured them one at a time. After each snap at the meat, he lifted his head and looking for an enemy. Luckily he was able to finish the whole meal.

Late in the afternoon, Kian started thinking about stopping for the evening. Some high cliffs on the east side of the river looked like they might afford him protection from predators. He flew close to the top and looked for a place to rest. He decided it would be better to stay at the top of the cliff instead of by the river. He couldn't imagine anything he should be afraid of, but his bird instincts put him close to the top. He wondered how scary it must have been for Raven if he had traveled through this part of the country and had to stop for the night.

That evening Kian found a short alder bush similar to the one he stayed on back at Lake Superior. This particular bush grew underneath a ridge that stuck out on the east side of the river. Because it was underneath the ridge, Kian was a little nervous, but not enough to want to find another place. He got comfortable and, since he was facing west, he hoped he would get to see a beautiful sunset.

The sun was just beginning to creep below the cloud bank in the west. The thin white streaks of the cirrus clouds intertwined with the fading red of the sun making the whole sky look like it was on fire. As the sun dropped below the distant trees, the colors changed from red to crimson and finally, with the onset of darkness, to a deep violet purple. Kian decided this was one of the prettiest sunsets he had ever seen.

~ ~ ~ ~ ~

Kian was shocked when the sleek cougar dropped from the ridge above him with its outstretched paw and sharp claws missing him by only inches. A few seconds lost in that beautiful sunset almost cost Kian his life.

As soon as the cougar landed, it immediately swung its left paw at Kian. The claw struck him below the left wing, just hard enough to knock him out of the bush, and against the granite rock. The cougar hesitated only a second before it jumped at Kian. Kian reacted more quickly and dodged the cougar, so the cougar hit the cliff just as Kian had.

As Kian stretched out his wings to take flight, the cougar slapped at one of them, pinning it against a rock near the edge of the cliff. Kian couldn't move. The cougar brought its head closer, mouth wide open, ready to rip Kian apart. He was intent on having Kian for his next meal. But just before the cougar sank its large pointed teeth into Kian's back, Kian turned his head all the way around and stabbed his sharp beak into the cougar's left eye.

It was just enough to make the cougar release Kian's trapped wing. When it did, Kian pushed off and dropped over the side of the cliff. The cougar took one last swing at him but missed completely. Kian was tumbling to the rocks that jutted out of the river when he realized he wasn't flying. For whatever the reason, Kian had both of his wings tucked in and was falling through the air like a rock.

Kian turned his head and tried to steady his body so that his beak was pointing straight down. He was moving through the air at an incredible speed. Shortly before he reached the rocks that stuck out of the river, Kian stretched out his wings and turned his head up, causing the wind to grab his delicate finger feathers. He soared parallel to the river instead of crashing into the rocks.

Kian spent the next fifteen minutes looking for a place to spend the night. When he finally found a tall tree at the top of the cliffs, he sat on a branch, looking at his wounds. He wasn't hurt badly, but the cougar had torn the flesh just above his left leg.

Kian wasn't sure how this could have happened. He realized if he had used his bird instincts and not thought about the sunset, he probably would have sensed the cougar and reacted more quickly. He needed to be more careful about when he could think like a boy and not like a bird. And he needed to be more careful about finding a place to stay at night, a place where it wouldn't be easy for a predator to capture him.

On the second day, Kian noticed the river was becoming very shallow and fewer cliffs lined its sides. He knew he was coming to the end of the river. Just as he had figured there was a lake that fed the river, Kian would have to decide which way Raven might have gone if, in fact, he had actually come this way and made it this far. So far, there had been no sign of him.

Kian sat in a large oak tree surveying the land encircling the lake. He decided to go high in the sky and circle the lake to watch for any signs a horse might have been there lately. For a long time he searched, hoping to find tracks or any other evidence Raven had gone this way. Weather would have erased tracks unless they had been made very recently. Besides, the ground was rocky and somewhat hard so the likelihood of tracks wasn't good.

He was flying close to the ground, feeling discouraged and ready to give up, when he spotted something that made him turn his head. He looked about fifty yards ahead of him, to his left. At first, he thought it was just another rock, but the coloring wasn't the same so he flew over to it.

As he got closer he realized that it wasn't just another rock. He knew exactly what it was. He had seen it many times before. It was dung. Raven's dung, he hoped. In the wintertime, and in places where there just wasn't much food, animal droppings could save a bird or a small animal's life. Many a bird has been known to peck through an animal's dung looking for undigested seeds or corn.

Kian swooped back around, deciding to investigate. While sifting through the pile of dung, he noticed another pile a short distance from the first. After carefully looking at both piles he realized the dung appeared to have straw mixed in it. Kian was quite sure the dung didn't belong to Raven, since there would have been no way Raven could have eaten straw or hay out here.

Kian continued to check out the area for other clues. Looking very closely, he thought he saw what appeared to be the footprint of a boot. As he looked at it, he also noticed animal prints on each side of the footprint. He wondered if two animals had stood there. Maybe one was Raven. It was all he had to go on. After studying the prints, he determined which way they were traveling and went in that direction, continuing on his journey.

~ 11 ~

Kian sat in a tree trying to decide what he would do for food when he thought he caught sight of movement way off on the horizon. At first he thought it was just the wind and the dust playing tricks on him but as he watched it more intensely he was sure something was out there. He couldn't tell what—maybe a couple of deer or bears. Whatever he saw appeared to be moving in the same direction he was. His heart began to race because it was the first time he had seen anything worthwhile since he set out on his journey.

Whoever they were and whatever they were doing didn't matter. He was just glad to see someone out here. He was about ready to give up on this whole journey. After watching from a distance, he decided to move up to investigate. He flew to a tree ahead of the movement and waited. The source of the movement soon became clear. It seemed an odd combination, the three of them: an old man, a mule, and a horse. The old man walked alongside the mule instead of riding the horse. The mule had everything packed on him. Nothing was on the horse. It almost looked like the horse was just tagging along. The boy instinct in him wondered if this might be Raven.

When they got closer yet, Kian could see the horse was a strong, sleek, beautiful, black animal. It held its head high and proud as it walked slowly next to the old man and the mule. Occasionally, it ran up ahead of the other two and then looked back as if to say, "Look at me!" Kian became excited. This could very well be Raven.

Waves of familiar feelings ran through Kian as they did when he first saw his father and Taza as a bird. The more he studied the horse, the more he knew it had to be Raven. The closer Raven came, the faster his heart, beat. Kian was sure he had found his long-lost friend. He wanted to jump out of the tree and fly right over and land on his back. He wanted to make the horse understand who he was, but he knew that it would never work.

He decided it would be best to watch him from a distance awhile, before getting too close. He flew high in the sky so he could observe the trio and remain undetected. Then he flew to a tree up ahead of them and watched as they approached. Kian figured the old man must have found Raven and was taking care of him.

He followed them as they made their way to a small farm, keeping his distance, so the old man wouldn't become curious why the bird was following them. Kian knew sooner or later he'd need to get close enough that both Raven and the old man would see him.

Kian, flying high, watched the three head west while they crested a hill. They began their descent to the farm. He saw a wide, old oak tree about two hundred yards from a house and shed. That might be the perfect place to stay while he figured out just what he was going to do.

His plan had always been to try and get Raven to go back with him to his father's farm. The only problem was, he didn't know how. He couldn't just fly up to the old man and say, "Excuse me, if it's okay with you I'd like to take the horse back to his owner." Even if he could talk, which he couldn't, the old man would never believe that. Kian knew about the only way he would get Raven back was to somehow get him to understand who he was. He had no idea how he would accomplish this.

So Kian stayed in the oak tree studying the beautiful black horse he was sure was Raven. As the trio approached the buildings, the mule went right into the shed as soon as the old man took the gear off its back, but the horse went to the side of the shed and stayed under a lean-to.

At first this didn't mean anything to Kian, but that evening, when the old man brought feed to the animals, the old man didn't bring the horse into the shed. He was going to let him stay out under the lean-to. The shed looked big enough to hold two animals, maybe even three. So, why wouldn't the old man let the horse stay in the shed? Could it be Raven didn't want to go in the shed? Maybe that was it.

Kian thought about this. He knew he still wasn't able to remember everything about his past. It seemed like he only remembered things in pieces. He remembered Taza said Raven ran away because of a storm, but what would that have to do with staying in the shed? No matter how hard he tried, he couldn't come up with a reason. Kian wasn't sure, but he thought all of this might have something to do with why Raven left their farm.

The second day Kian spent in the oak tree, he got to observe Raven up close. The old man brought Raven over to the field where the old oak tree stood and turned him loose. As soon as the old man removed Raven's halter, he took off in a full gallop across the field. He ran within fifteen feet of the oak tree, and Kian got a really good look at the beauty and strength of him. Kian wanted to fly down and ride Raven but realized it was not the right time.

As the horse raced by the tree a second time, Kian's memory of the horse turned from recognition of a beautiful animal to remembering him as his friend. He wondered if Raven still shared the same memory of him. Did Raven still think of him as his friend? Did he even remember Kian? He wanted to go to Raven and find out, but he was a bird, not a boy. Raven would have no way of knowing who he was. So he stayed in the tree, watching.

The old man went back to the house to go about his daily chores. Raven ran through the field a couple more times and then came to a stop about fifty feet from the tree. He stood there awhile, then he noticed the shady spot under the tree. He ambled over to it. He stopped directly under the branch Kian was sitting on.

Kian's heart raced as it had when his grandfather walked over to the fence on which he had perched. Kian realized his bird instinct made his heart race. He stretched out his wings like he was going to take flight, but didn't. Raven looked up and saw him but was not interested in a bird, so he looked back down and started munching the tall grass.

Kian admired Raven. Now he could remember all the good times he'd shared with Raven. He remembered how he used to ride him bareback and how it felt to have the wind blowing in his face as they galloped at high speed across the open range in front of their farm. All those wonderful memories came flooding back to him, and he wanted things to be back the way they were before . . . before the storm.

The gray, dark cloud of the storm washed away all the good memories, and Kian started to think about why he had come here in the first place. He realized things could not be the way they used to be, because *he* was not who he used to be.

Kian stretched his long black wings again and this time took to the air. He flapped his wings hard so that he could gain lots of speed. The thought of not being able to be with Raven made him angry, and he wanted to get away from his friend. He didn't know if he could go through with his plan to try and get Raven back with his father. The more he thought about it, the faster he flew.

He flew low to the ground and spotted a large rock up ahead. He thought, *Why don't I just fly right into that rock?* But the bird instinct took over, and when he came within just a few feet of the rock he pulled his head up and flew over it, missing it by inches. Why couldn't he just be himself again? Why did he have to be a stupid bird? He wanted to be a boy again and be with Pop-o and Raven.

When his anger finally left him, he flew back to the same branch above Raven. When he landed, Raven never even looked up. Kian began to realize the best he could hope for was to somehow get Raven to go back to his father's farm and hope his father would quit drinking and get his life back to normal. Kian knew his own life would never be the same.

The next day Kian was flying high, almost a quarter of a mile from the tree, when he saw the old man bring Raven and the mule (which Kian had heard was named One Eye) over to the field where Raven had run the day before. Kian wondered if the old man was going to take them on a trip again. The old man turned Raven loose and tied One Eye to the fence. Apparently, he didn't trust One Eye well enough to let him run free.

Raven took off across the field at a full gallop, just as he had the day before. The old man didn't stay to watch, so Kian decided to drop down and let Raven see him. He dropped his right wing and moved in behind

Raven, keeping a reasonable distance between them. He wanted to wait until Raven got to the far end of the field before he let Raven see him.

Raven must have sensed something behind him, because all of a sudden he came to a quick stop and turned his head to look behind. He stopped so quickly Kian almost flew right into Raven's rear end, but with one swift movement of his head and a slight twist of his finger feathers, Kian went up and over Raven almost before Raven could see him.

Kian landed on a small rock about twenty feet in front of Raven. He turned around and saw Raven staring back at him. Kian couldn't help but wonder what Raven was thinking. The two stood looking at each other for a long time. For a moment Kian thought maybe Raven would take off running, but Raven had no reason to be afraid—confused, maybe—but not afraid.

When Raven didn't take off running, Kian thought maybe Raven had recognized him. Of course, Kian only thought this for a second, then remembered he was a bird, not the boy Raven would have remembered

As Kian stood on the rock, staring at Raven, Raven must have wanted to get a better look. As the horse moved closer to him, Kian was sure Raven had never been in a situation like this before.

Kian spread his wings but didn't fly away. Slowly, Raven walked toward him. When Raven got within five feet of Kian, the bird instinct made him jump off the rock and back up a few steps, so, Raven stopped. It was a very awkward situation for both of them.

They were a long ways away from the old man, so when the old man whistled for Raven, Kian was sure the old man couldn't see him and decided not to fly away when Raven turned around and headed back to the fence. He just waited on the rock and watched as Raven trotted back. He felt at least he had made a connection with Raven.

The next day, Kian was flying back to the tree after visiting the old man's cornfield. A few of the stalks had been knocked down, so Kian was able to get something to eat. As he approached the tree, he saw that the old man must have let Raven out to run again because the horse was standing under the tree, almost as if he was waiting for Kian to return.

Rather than land on a branch in the tree, Kian decided to land on the ground in front of Raven. The landing startled Raven and he tossed his head and backed up a little. The two looked at each other for a minute. Then Raven turned and galloped away. He only went about thirty yards before he turned and began to circle the tree. The whole time Kian sat on the ground, watching.

After Raven circled the tree three times, Kian got an idea and took off. When Raven saw him take off, he turned and headed toward the far end of the field. Kian followed. After they had gone about a hundred yards, Kian flapped his wings harder and caught up with Raven. He flew directly over Raven's rear end, about a foot above it.

Kian's idea was to land on Raven while he was running. Slowly, he dropped his legs down, being careful not to hurt Raven with his claws. When they gently touched Raven's back, Raven turned his head and looked but continued to run. After a few seconds, Kian was able to draw in his wings and land. He was actually riding Raven.

After a few more minutes of running, Raven came to a stop. Kian continued to sit on Raven's back. Raven turned his head to look at him, but it didn't bother Kian. It appeared Raven was perfectly fine with him. Kian was fairly sure Raven didn't know who he was, but he also knew Raven accepted him as a friend.

Kian looked back toward the house and noticed that the old man and One Eye were both standing next to the fence, watching them. He couldn't help but wonder what the old man thought. When the old man whistled, Raven turned and started toward the fence. Kian decided this wasn't the time to meet the old man, so he took off and headed for the oak tree. He'd get another chance to be with Raven later and he was sure sooner or later he'd meet the old man.

Kian was sitting in the tree late the next morning, wondering why the old man hadn't let Raven out for a run. Could it be that the old man was concerned about Raven and the bird being together? That didn't make sense. What possible harm could come from the bird riding the horse? Maybe the old man just wasn't going to let Raven run every day.

Finally, Kian decided that, if Raven couldn't come to the tree, he'd go visit Raven at the lean-to. He jumped off the branch, flapped his wings and headed for the shed. From a distance he could see Raven was eating from his feed trough, which reminded Kian he hadn't eaten anything since the day before and was hungry himself.

He landed on the end of the wooden trough, only about two feet away from Raven's head. It startled Raven. The horse jerked its head from the trough and took a step backward. When Raven saw who it was, he shook his head a couple of times and went back to eating. Raven seemed not the least bit concerned about the bird.

Kian noticed corn mullet in with the feed mix and knew it might be some time before he got another chance to eat. He decided to have some of the mullet. He moved over a little on the edge of the trough and began to peck away at it. Raven looked up once at the bird, but it seemed as though he could care less. They both continued eating for some time, and then all of a sudden the old man came around the corner of the shed and saw the two of them.

"Well, would you look at that?" he said out loud. "I'll be danged if that horse hasn't found himself a friend."

The old man stood watching Kian and Raven eat at the trough. Kian had seen the old man come around the corner, but he was far enough away he wasn't too concerned. He kept his eye on him as he continued to dig through the feed in search of more corn mullet.

When Raven had finished eating, he lifted his head from the trough and backed up a couple of steps. Kian continued to eat as the old man walked over to Raven and stroked his neck.

"So, are you going to tell me who your new friend is? Or is he an old friend from your past who's finally found you?" The old man said it like he expected an answer, but Raven just lifted his head. Then the old man turned to the bird.

"How about you? Have you got anything worth 'crowing' about? What's with this strange relationship between you and the horse? I've seen you around the past couple of days and wondered if you'd ever have enough nerve to meet me."

The old man finally led Raven over to the field and turned him loose. Raven ran straight for the oak tree. Kian took off after him, reaching the tree first and landing on a branch. Raven stopped under the branch. Kian wondered if he was waiting for him to get on his back. He jumped down from the branch and gently landed on Raven's back. It was almost like Raven knew exactly what to do and took off, first at a slow trot, but he gradually picked up speed until he was at a full run with Kian still on his back.

Raven ran through the grass and around the trees. He ran all the way down to the far end of the property and back, with Kian stuck to his back the whole time. They appeared to be playing. And while this was going on, the old man stood by the fence watching.

The next morning, Kian sat on the limb of the huge oak tree holding a small jack rabbit under his foot. He was almost ready to let the rest of the mangled body drop to the ground when he noticed there was a pretty good-sized piece of meat still on the leg so he began to tear at it with his sharp beak. He wished there was more, but whatever animal had caught the rabbit had eaten most of the meat. It had been awhile since he had eaten a really good meal so he savored every morsel. He realized it didn't bother him any more when he found a dead animal for food and wondered if he was becoming more a bird and less a boy. The more he thought about that, the less he liked it.

The whole time that he had been eating he was trying to figure how he could get Raven back to his father. He knew he couldn't just go up and whisper the idea in Raven's ear and expect Raven to just nod his head and follow him. He realized the only way to get him there would be if he could somehow convince Raven to follow him. So far, Raven had trusted him enough to let him ride on his back. But to follow him away from the security and safety of the old man—that would be a bit trickier.

The next day the old man let Raven run loose, as usual. Raven looked around the field but must not have spotted Kian, so he trotted over to the tree. Kian was on a branch high in the tree. Raven stood under the tree awhile, then walked around almost as though he was looking for the bird. The old man stood by the fence watching, then went about his business.

Kian had decided if the old man didn't see him with Raven, he would probably go about his business, hopefully go back in the house. He wanted to be alone with Raven in hopes of luring him away. He figured it would be easier to get Raven to leave the property if the old man wasn't in sight. It was a long shot, but Kian had to try something.

The old man did go back into the house. Kian waited a few minutes until Raven had walked a pretty good distance from the tree. Kian jumped from the tree and flew toward Raven, staying close to the ground. He came up behind him, passed him, and then flew about fifty yards ahead of him and landed on the ground. When Raven saw him he trotted after him. The horse came to a stop just before he got to Kian, and as soon as he stopped, Kian took off and flew another fifty yards ahead. Raven followed.

Kian did this several more times, and each time Raven followed, never looking back to see how far they had gotten from the farm. When they were over a half-mile away from the house, Raven came to a stop and turned around as if to see where they were. Kian had already taken off for the next fifty-yard move. When he landed, he noticed Raven had not followed him this time. He was looking back at the house which was now just a small dot on the horizon.

For the longest time Raven stood there, looking back. He turned to look at Kian one time, then turned back and looked at the house, probably looking for the old man. But they were so far away now he couldn't see him, even if the old man had been outside. At one point Raven turned toward the house and took a step in that direction. He stopped and turned back to look at Kian. It was obvious he wasn't sure what he should do.

When he looked at him, Kian flapped his wings and gave a loud screech as if to say, "Come on!" Raven didn't move. He just stood there. Kian jumped in the air and flew another ten feet hoping that would get Raven to follow, but he just stood there looking puzzled.

If Raven headed back to the house, Kian's chances of getting Raven to follow him back to his father's place would be over. Raven trusted him, but following him all the way back to their farm was a lot to expect.

As Kian watched, Raven took one step, then another back toward the old man's house, looking back at Kian with each step. Kian wanted so much for Raven to follow him, but there just wasn't anything he could do. Finally, Kian decided to leave. He couldn't bear to watch Raven head back to the old man's house. He realized he had done all he could to get Raven to come back with him, and Raven had made his decision.

This time when he took off, he flew almost straight up. When he reached a high altitude, he dropped his right wing and his long sleek body straightened out. He was ready to start the journey back to Lake Superior, but he thought he'd better watch Raven for a short while in case Raven did turn around and try to follow him. If he didn't, Kian knew the only thing left for him to do would be to head back to the cliffs of Lake Superior and begin the rest of his life as a bird. He hoped he would be able to forget about all of this. Maybe, in time, it would all be forgotten.

He kept his wings rigid with his finger feathers spread apart so he could soar in big circles as he watched his friend Raven continued slowly back to the fence. His bird instinct told him he should get moving so he might find a safe place for the night, since he'd never make it all the way back to the cliffs by sunset, but the boy in him said go back to Raven one more time and see if he would follow.

The bird instinct won out, and Kian headed back. He saw Raven still walking very slowly in the direction of the old man's house. Going back one more time would do no good. Raven was doing what he felt was in his best interests and now Kian had to do the same.

~ 12 ~

It had only been about five minutes since the two had gone their separate ways. Kian was flying high and slow. He really wasn't in a big hurry. He knew he wouldn't make it back to Lake Superior for at least another day. When he turned slightly to the right out of habit he looked back, knowing Raven should no longer be in sight.

He had just started to turn back homeward when something caught his eye. It looked like a small cloud of dust near the horizon behind him. He dropped a wing and turned his body to face the cloud for a better look. All he could see was the dust. After staring at it long enough, he realized Raven was galloping at full speed toward him. Kian dropped his head, flapped both wings hard, and flew straight for his friend—flying so fast his eyes began to water.

Kian approached Raven, flying low so Raven would see him coming, then turned around and flew to a large rock about a hundred yards ahead of him. Raven slowed and came to a stop right in front of Kian.

Kian couldn't communicate directly with Raven, but it appeared that, instinctively, Raven knew what Kian wanted. Kian couldn't help but wonder if Raven actually knew who he was, but he dismissed the thought when he realized it didn't matter. The important thing was getting Raven safely back to the farm.

Kian began leading Raven home. He had thought about this several times in the past few days. The trip would be easy for him. He could fly. He would need to find the safest, easiest, quickest way for Raven back to the farm.

Kian only knew two ways back—other than flying. The first was the way he had come, following the river. If he chose to go that way, it would be difficult for Raven because walking next to the river could be rough terrain. There would also be less food for Raven that way. The other way was to follow the old logger's trail which weaved in and out of the forest. The trail ended a short distance from the cliffs on Lake Superior where the river ended. The logger's trail was probably the easiest and safest way, but it would take at least a day longer to get to where they were going.

Kian knew Raven had traveled one of these routes, so he decided to see which one Raven would take back. He led Raven to the point where they would need to either turn southeast and follow the river or go due east and follow the logger's trail. When he got there, he sat on a rock, hoping Raven would continue one way or the other. Raven just stood there, waiting for Kian to move. After a long enough wait, Kian decided to try something else. He flew off the rock and landed on Raven's back and sat there. It only took a minute for Raven to understand what Kian wanted. Raven headed southeast toward the river with Kian firmly on his back.

When they got to the river, Kian jumped off of Raven's back and flew to one of the rocks ahead and watched Raven. He wondered if Raven would walk along the edge of the river or go into the river where it was deep enough and swim. Kian noticed that the current flowed in the direction that they would be traveling making it easy for Raven to swim. He could probably just float most of the way. He watched as Raven made his way into the river.

For the rest of the day Kian would fly a long ways ahead of Raven and then sit on a tall rock or on one of the cliffs and watch as Raven came floating down the river. Once he flew high into the sky and looked down at Raven as he continued to float. Kian was so high that, when he saw Raven, he looked like a bobber floating in a stream. Kian found a dead fish washed up from the river and tore it apart, looking for anything still edible. He felt bad when Raven floated by and saw him eating the fish because he knew there wasn't much food out here for Raven.

They spent the first night in an alcove-like cave alongside of the river, but the entrance merely came to a dead end. It didn't matter though. It was still a good place for Raven to bed down for the night. Kian, of course, spent the night in a tall pine a short distance from the alcove, watching over Raven.

Late in the second day, Kian was beginning to wonder if they should find a place to stop for the night. He was sitting high on a cliff, almost a quarter of a mile down river from Raven. He noticed Raven was coming out of the water and wondered why he was stopping. The river appeared to be plenty wide, and there weren't many rapids, so he couldn't understand why Raven wouldn't just keep floating.

Raven just stood on the bank of the river and waited. *What's he doing*, Kian thought. *Why isn't he continuing down the side of the river?* Finally, Kian understood that it must be the place where Raven had entered the river when he left the farm. *That must be another way to get back*, Kian thought, and flew over to Raven, who was already heading down a narrow path that led into some tall pine trees.

~ ~ ~ ~ ~

Kian stood on a large boulder at the start of the trail that led to Lake Superior. He had been there several times before but as a boy, not a bird. Many of his memories were coming back to him, and he wasn't sure he liked that. He and Raven had made it through the pine trees that led from the river. They had followed the rugged, narrow trail for almost a day and were now close to the place he had gone with his grandfather to learn about the Magic Sunrise, the place that he had gone to ask the spirits to help him find Raven, the place where he had . . . fallen from the broken rock. They were not all good memories.

But today they would not be following that trail. They would go the other way, to Kian's father's farm, where he hoped the return of Raven would help his father deal with the pain of losing his son.

Kian stood on the fence post as he watched Raven looking at the terrain in front of him. Raven was on the other side of the road looking down the long dirt path that led to their property. He could clearly see the house and shed, even though they were a quarter of a mile away.

Kian couldn't help but wonder if Raven knew this used to be his home, that it used to be home for both of them. He had no way of being sure, but he hoped Raven knew enough about this place that he would stay.

After a few moments of looking over the property, Raven stepped out onto the road and crossed it. He hesitated for only a few seconds, then took off down the path at a full gallop. Raven must have recognized the place and was now in a hurry to return.

Kian felt confused. He wasn't sure how he should be feeling. He was happy Raven seemed to recognize the place, knowing there was a good chance Raven would stay and things would be better for his father, but Kian also felt empty.

Now that it looked like he had accomplished what he had set out to do, Kian began to realize this could very well be the end of the relationship between him and Raven. He also felt bad he would never get to do all the things a boy his age got to do.

More than anything else, though, Kian was sad, sad because he knew there was no way he could be with his father again, sad because he wouldn't be able to ride Raven—at least, not as a boy. He also missed his grandfather. All of these feelings were bottled up inside Kian at the same time.

He wondered if the best thing to do was leave and forget about Raven altogether. Sooner or later he would have to do that, but this just didn't seem like the right time, not yet, anyway. He looked toward the farm and then back at the road leading to Lake Superior, not knowing what to do.

Kian took off from the fence post and headed high into the sky. He decided he wanted to stay as distant as he could while watching Raven, to find out if he would make the transition back to the farm, to see how his father would react.

He stayed in the air, circling the property, watching as Raven ran the rest of the way down the dirt path, to the house. The truck wasn't in the yard, so Kian was pretty sure nobody was at home.

When Raven made it to the house, he stood by the porch for a minute and then walked over to the shed. Kian realized Raven wouldn't recognize the shed. It was much smaller than the one the storm destroyed. It looked like it was only half as big—just big enough for one horse.

A neighing from inside the shed let Kian know Morton must have sensed Raven was out there. When Morton finished neighing, Raven answered him. So far, things seemed to be going the way Kian had hoped they would.

Raven walked over to the fence line next to Mrs. Harris's garden and nibbled on the grasses that grew near the posts. Kian had thought about checking out the corn on the other side of her house but decided against it. He wanted to be on the roof when the truck pulled up so he wouldn't draw attention to himself.

It seemed a long time before Kian finally saw the cloud of dust chasing the truck as it made its way down the old dirt road. He knew it was Pop-o, and his heart began to race. He thought about the last time he was here, before he went to look for Raven. He remembered how his father kept the bottle in the house instead of hiding it in the shed, how Pop-o had set the bottle down on the kitchen table like it was perfectly fine to drown his sorrows since nobody was around. He knew his father would never have done that if he was still there. That made Kian feel bad, almost like it was his fault his father had gone back to drinking.

Raven must have seen the truck turn down the path also, because he quit eating and walked over to wait by the shed. When Kian's father was halfway down the path, the truck came to a stop. Kian's father must have spotted Raven. The truck didn't move for a long time, and then it finally continued to the house, but very slowly. When the truck finally stopped, a short distance from the front porch, Kian's father got out, never taking his eyes off of Raven.

"Raven, is that you, Raven?" was all he said.

He walked over to the animal and stroked his neck, all the time keeping his face very close to Raven's head, almost like he was whispering something to him. Kian was too far away to tell if he was talking to him or not. He was perched on the top of the house, but on the furthest roofline from the porch, so he couldn't be seen. He wanted to stay completely out of the picture.

A deafening silence throughout the farm lasted as long as Raven stood still while Kian's father stroked his neck. Kian's father finally broke down and started to cry. He wept hard and long, all the time burying his face in Raven's neck.

Then he backed away from Raven and spoke in a loud, harsh voice. "What are you doing here? Why did you come back?" he yelled. "Don't you know Kian isn't here? Don't you know what it did to him when you left?" He stopped just long enough to wipe the tears from his eyes. "And now you show up here like nothing happened. Well, he's not here. Do you understand, he's not here and he never will be . . . he's gone forever."

Kian watched as his father turned around and walked into the house, slamming the door behind him.

Kian felt hurt and even more confused. He thought bringing Raven back would make his father happy. Instead it made him angry. Why was his father mad at Raven? It wasn't his fault.

Raven walked over behind the shed, where he was protected from the wind. It would be sunset soon, and Kian decided he needed to figure out what he was going to do. He wished he could explain to his father that everything would be all right. He wanted his father to be happy.

He flew down from the roof onto a fence post close enough to the house for him to look into the kitchen window. There on the kitchen table stood a half-empty bottle of whiskey and a glass. Next to it sat Kian's father with his head buried in his arms.

This was too much for Kian. He flew from the fence post to the roof of the shed. He'd spend the night close to Raven. He needed time to think. He began to doubt if he had done the right thing by bringing Raven back. He wondered if Raven's return gave his father memories too hard for him to deal with. Would it have been better to leave Raven where he found him? Would his father feel differently about Raven tomorrow and want him to stay? He decided to give his father a couple of days to see if he was better off with or without Raven on the farm.

The next day, late in the morning, Kian's father came out of the house to feed Morton and Raven. Kian wondered if he had been up most of the night drinking. Was he drowning his sorrows for losing his wife and then losing his son in a freak accident? His father was probably at the lowest point in his life, and all of a sudden the horse that belonged to his wife and son had returned from nowhere.

Kian wished his father could understand that the horse had been sent to help take away his pain and ease his sorrows. That this was a sign from the spirits above that Kian was okay. He needed to understand they were trying to tell him it was time for him to get on with his life and remember Kian through Raven.

That morning, Kian thought Raven looked tired. He remained lying on the ground behind the shed even after the sun was up. Kian flew over to Mrs. Harris's garden for some breakfast. When he came back, Raven was still on the ground. He wondered if Raven was tired from the long trip, or if he sensed what was going on with Kian's father. Kian flew over to Raven and landed on his back in hopes he'd get up and go for a run. He didn't.

While Raven was still on the ground with Kian on his back, Kian's father rounded the corner of the shed and saw the two of them. Kian's father became upset immediately, probably because he thought something had happened to Raven.

"What have you done to my horse!" he yelled. "Get off of him and get out of here."

When the bird didn't move, Pop-o charged toward it, waving his arms. "Can't you hear, you dumb bird? Get out of here and leave us alone!"

Kian jumped off of Raven and flew to a fence post next to the shed. The post was out of sight so Pop-o couldn't see him. Pop-o noticed Raven's water trough was empty. Worried that Raven might be dehydrated from his journey, Pop-o picked up a bucket, and headed to the pump alongside the house for water. He wondered how Raven could look so good after being gone this long. *Someone must have been taking care of him,* he thought. He hoped Raven was only tired and not sick.

When Pop-o left, Kian looked at Raven, wishing there was something he could do to make their family whole again. Once again, Kian had those confused mixed feelings running through him, and he wasn't sure what to do. One part of him wanted to stay, but another part of him knew he couldn't. *If only my father knew who I really was,* thought Kian.

Kian finally realized there would never be a way he could get his father to understand who he was and why he was here. Now that his father had at least accepted Raven, there was nothing else for him to do but leave.

He walked all the way down the fence to the gate, and then turned around and came back to look at Raven for probably the last time. He knew how hard this was going to be, but once he left, he didn't plan to come back. All he could do was hope Raven's presence would lessen the pain for his father.

Kian was just getting ready to take flight when he heard Pop-o's footsteps in back of him. "Are you still here? I thought I told you to leave." Kian could tell he was upset—really upset. "Well, you apparently don't understand words, but maybe you'll understand this."

Pop-o searched the ground for a few seconds and found what he was looking for. He picked the rock up and threw it yelling, "Now get out of here and stay out!"

Kian took to the air when he saw Pop-o bend over and pick up the rock. He knew it was time to leave and wondered if he might have stayed too long. Flying just above the shack, the rock hit his right wing knocking off two of his flight feathers. He immediately lost control and started to drop. Falling from the sky, he was almost able to clear the back of the shed roof—but not quite— and as he fell he hit his head on the edge of the roof. Unconscious, he fell into a pile of straw next to Raven.

~ ~ ~ ~ ~

Kian was just able to open one of his eyes as his father rounded the corner of the shed. He took a few steps toward Kian and Raven, then came to a sudden stop. Pop-o's eyes opened wide and stared as if he couldn't believe what he saw. *Why is he staring at me?* Kian thought, *Is something wrong with me?* Kian shut his eyes and passed out.

~ 13 ~

The next thing that Kian remembered was waking in his bed. He tried to open his eyes but couldn't. Something cool was on his forehead and it covered his eyes too. He heard voices and knew it must be Pop-o and his grandfather. They were speaking so softly Kian could barely hear what they were saying. He wasn't sure, but he thought he heard them say something about a bird.

When Pop-o noticed Kian stirring, he and Taza stepped out of the room into the hall.

". . . Like I said, I threw a rock at the raven to scare it off. I must have hit its wing because it fell down behind the shed. When I got to the back of the shed, Kian was lying next to Raven in the straw with a big knot on his head. There wasn't any bird."

Taza rubbed his chin and asked, "Is it possible Kian had been lying there, next to Raven, all night and you just didn't see him?"

"I don't think so. I don't remember seeing him," he paused for a moment, then continued, "I know this doesn't make any sense, but I'm telling you what happened. You do believe me, don't you? I'm not going crazy, am I?" Kian's father pleaded with Taza.

The two of them stood in silence a long time. Finally, Taza looked at Pop-o and spoke in a very soft voice. "Yes, I do believe you, as crazy as this seems. I can't tell you how the spirits of our ancestors work, but at times they can play a very important role in the way we survive. They will only affect the ones who truly believe in their powers. Kian believed in the spirits with his whole heart. Maybe this is their way of answering him.

"I don't know how Kian ended up next to Raven. Maybe he came with him and you didn't see him. Maybe he came in the night. And as for that bird, well, a raven paid me a visit a while ago. Something about him made me wonder if he wasn't trying to tell me something, so I told him about Raven and Kian. The bird sat on the fence and listened the whole time. When I finished, he flew away.

"It doesn't really matter how or why this happened. What matters is Kian's back. Now we must go on from here. It isn't important to understand the 'why' of the spirits. What's important is believing in them and accepting what they've done."

Pop-o nodded in agreement with Taza, and then said, "How much of this do you think he'll remember?"

"I don't know," Taza answered. "Probably none of it. We'll cross that bridge when we come to it. He may never ask us anything. Let's just . . ."

Before he could finish, Kian groaned, and the two of them went back into his room. Kian had pulled the washcloth from his eyes. At first he didn't say anything. He just lay there looking at the ceiling. Finally, he turned his head and looked into his father's eyes and smiled.

"Pop-o. Oh, Pop-o, I just had the weirdest dream." Then he turned his head a little further and saw Taza standing near the foot of the bed. "Grandpa, what are you doing here? Do you want to hear my dream too?"

Kian's father and Taza both laughed. A tear ran down Pop-o's cheek as he bent down and gave his son a kiss on the forehead. Taza grabbed Kian's hand and squeezed it. Kian couldn't understand why they both seemed so happy to see him.

Kian looked at the two of them like they were both crazy and said, "What?" That just made both of them laugh all the harder.

Kian remembered very little about what had happened. He wasn't sure if what he remembered was real or fantasy. He remembered Raven had run away because of a storm, and that maybe he and his father went to look for him but couldn't find him. In his dream, he said, Raven had found his way home by flying high in the sky and looking all over until he finally saw the farm. Then he landed and was lying down behind the shed, and Pop-o was next to him, crying.

"And then I woke up," Kian said. "Isn't that a weird dream, Pop-o?"

"Yes, Kian, that does sound a little strange. But you've got to remember we're not always supposed to understand our dreams. Sometimes a dream tells us a story about our past or our future, but we're unable to understand it until later in our life. When you get older, this dream may make more sense to you."

Kian was puzzled. *I wonder what he means by that,* he thought. Then he said, "When I get older, will you talk to me about this dream again?"

"When you get older we will talk about a lot of things, my son."

Kian's father told Kian he needed to get some more rest. He said he would come back in a little while and bring him something to eat. Kian closed his eyes and fell fast asleep.

The next morning Kian woke up early and heard his father moving around on the front porch. He wrapped his blanket around his shoulders and made his way down the steps. He stood in the doorway and watched his father for a moment before stepping out. His father was sitting on the porch rail, drinking a cup of coffee, looking out toward the distant pine trees. Kian wondered how long he had been sitting there.

"Pop-o, is everything okay?" Kian asked.

He must have startled his father because Pop-o sort of jumped backwards a little spilling some of his coffee. Kian thought it looked funny, the way his father jumped back, and he giggled.

"Oh, you scared me," Pop-o said. "What are you doing up so early?"

"I don't know. I guess I just couldn't sleep anymore."

There was a moment of awkward silence and then his father said, "Yes, Kian, everything is okay. In fact, everything is more than okay—it's terrific."

Pop-o slid off the porch rail, walked over to the bench and sat down. He motioned for Kian to come sit with him. When Kian did, Pop-o picked him up and put him in his lap like he used to when Kian was a small boy, then put his arm around him and gave him a big squeeze.

"You're not too big to sit in your Pop-o's lap are you?"

Kian giggled and snuggled his head against his father's chest, "Nooo! I'll never be too big for that."

"You look much better today. How do you feel?"

"I feel better than yesterday," he said.

Once again there was that awkward silence, and Kian wondered if Pop-o had something on his mind. Pop-o finally spoke again and seemed to choose his words carefully.

"Son, ever since your mother died, I haven't been . . . well I haven't been doing the best job as a father."

Kian started to object, but Pop-o held up his hand and said, "Now let me finish. When your mother died, it hurt me a great deal. I guess I tried to fix that hurt by drinking. I know you know about it, Kian, and I'm sorry."

Pop-o took a deep breath and went on. "When I thought I'd lost you and Raven, well, I thought it was the end of the world and . . . well, the drinking got worse. But, now that we're back together again, I promise, no more drinking."

Kian wanted to say something but he couldn't. He knew how hard it must have been for Pop-o to tell him that. All Kian could do was wipe the tears that had started to pour down his cheeks by burying his face in Pop-o's chest. Finally, he was able to whisper, "I love you, Pop-o."

Kian smiled when he heard his father answer, "I love you too, son."

It wasn't long and Kian was up and around, as good as new. At first he just helped around the house, but soon he was doing all the chores he had done in the past. He didn't ask his father too much about what had happened, but he knew there was a void in his life that someday would need to be filled. For now, though, he was just glad to be back.

He and Raven were beginning to get to know each other again. At first Raven acted strange toward everyone. It was almost like he wasn't familiar with the farm at all. Kian realized Raven would need time and gave him space. He let Raven run free on the farm, but Kian just couldn't wait until his father would let him ride Raven again.

It only took a couple of weeks before everything at the farm was pretty much normal. Kian's father once again began working long hours in town, just as he had done in the past, and that left Kian to tend to the cattle and the chores. Every night Kian would have supper ready for Pop-o when he got home, and the two would talk about what they had done all day.

Kian was sure his concussion was fully healed and he was ready to ride Raven again. He pestered his father regularly about it until Pop-o finally gave in and said it was okay. Kian was smart enough to wait a few days before he asked about riding bareback. When he did, he was surprised that his father had no objections.

Now that Raven was back, the shed would need to be extended so both Raven and Morton had a place to stay at night. Raven seemed perfectly fine staying outside, next to the shed, but Kian knew when the cold and snow of winter came, it would not be good for Raven to stay outside. Kian was not quite big enough to take on a project that size alone, so his grandfather came each day to help him. The project was good for both Kian and his grandfather because it gave the two of them a chance to re-kindle the relationship they had had before Kian disappeared.

~ ~ ~ ~ ~

Summer turned to fall, and Kian knew soon it would be time for the Magic Sunrise. He had spoken to Taza about it while they were working one day, and Taza told him that this year he would bring Kian to that special place on Lake Superior so he too could witness the beauty of the Magic Sunrise.

"Do you think Pop-o would go with us?" Kian asked, hoping that Taza would say yes.

"I know he is pretty busy this time of year, but he might if *you* asked him."

Kian knew just the right time to ask him, after a nice supper of fish, wild rice, and greens . . . and of course cornbread. Kian made the whole meal himself. His father put down his fork and smiled after he finished the last bite of cornbread.

"You did a fine job with supper tonight, Kian, a really fine job."

Kian thanked his father, and asked him how his day had gone. He slowly worked in the conversation about watching the Magic Sunrise with Taza.

Finally, Kian said, "We were wondering if maybe you . . ."

Before he could finish the sentence, Pop-o jumped in, "I was wondering if I was ever going to get invited. Of course I'll go with you. I can hardly wait."

~ ~ ~ ~ ~

The night was illuminated by an almost full moon that was descending in the western sky as Kian, Pop-o and Taza made their way down the path toward Lake Superior. Kian could tell by the small amount of light that was beginning to creep up in the eastern horizon that they would need to hurry if they expected to be there at just the right time.

When they reached the trail that led to the top of the cliffs, Kian slid off Raven's back and stroked his neck, then whispered in his ear.

"Do you want to come with me, Raven? You can wait here if you like but the last time we were here you came with me all the way to the top. Is it okay with you, Pop-o?"

His father looked at Taza, who rolled his eyes and shrugged, then nodded, and Raven tossed his large head backward as if he were nodding too, then pushed his nose against Kian's side, nudging him forward. Kian had no problem understanding what Raven was trying to tell him and continued up the path, his friend right behind him.

When they reached the top, Kian noticed the eastern sky was much brighter now and knew it would soon be time. Kian had waited a long time for this exact moment, and he was glad that he would be able to share it with both his father and his grandfather . . . and of course Raven, his best friend in the whole world.

He stood facing the peninsula and noticed the arch, jutting out of the side of one of the cliffs. He remembered the first time he saw that arch. It was with Taza—what seemed like a long time ago—and that was when he first heard the story about the Magic Sunrise.

He turned to Raven, who seemed more interested in a clump of weeds that had made their way through the rocky surface despite the terrible conditions for anything growing up there. "Raven, it's almost time. Pay attention to that arch on the distant horizon. Remember, the Magic Sunrise will only happen four days a year, and today is one of the days, right, Grandpa?"

His grandfather nodded, and then sat down on a rock, waiting for the show to begin. Raven looked up as if to acknowledge what Kian had said, but soon returned to the weeds.

Kian turned back to the arch and saw that the middle of the arch was beginning to get brighter. He glanced over to some of the other cliffs to the west and noticed that in some places the sun was already leaving its mark. Then he remembered what his grandfather had once told him. *Even though it may not be sunrise here, it's sunrise somewhere else.* Now Kian had a better understanding of what his grandfather had meant.

He turned back to the arch just in time to see the first ray of sunshine, peeping through the opening of the arch. It was just a trickle at first, but within seconds it began to fill the entire arch with a magnificent, golden color that immersed Kian in bright sunlight. He closed his eyes and let the sun bathe his face, but only for a second because he didn't want to miss any of the spectacular show.

"Isn't it beautiful?"

"Yes, it is. It's magnificent!" his father answered.

Within a few short minutes, the brilliance of the sunburst was already beginning to weaken. Kian turned and looked at his shadow and saw that it, too, was starting to fade. Once again he remembered what his grandfather had said. *Remember, Kian, you must be there right at sunrise because it will only last a very short time.* Kian hadn't understood then exactly what his grandfather meant, but now he did.

He watched as the last glimmer of light seeped through the opening, and finally the sun was out of sight, completely hidden behind the top of the arch. He knew the sun would again show its beauty when it came up over of the top of the arch, but that wouldn't be nearly as magnificent as the Magic Sunrise. When it came up again it would be just like every other sunrise. Not like this one, for this was indeed a *Magic Sunrise*.

Now that it was over, Kian turned to Raven and said, "Well, boy, what did you think of that?" Of course, Raven just continued munching the weeds. Raven might have been his best friend, but when it came to watching a sunrise, he was still just a horse.

Kian turned to look at the seemingly calm water on Lake Superior. When he heard the crashing waves below him he glanced over the edge of the cliff, not far from where he was standing. He remembered that the last time he was here with his grandfather there was a huge piece of rock that jutted out over the cliff. The huge rock had broken off and left the edge of the cliff looking bare.

It looks like it must have broken off recently, he thought.

He looked at Pop-o and Taza, who also appeared to be interested in the edge of the cliff and jokingly said, "I sure hope nobody was standing on that rock when it broke off."